Blue Water

The Nike Augustine Series

Book One

By M. L. Bullock

Dedication

Swim, little brother. I'm right behind you.

"Come this way, honored Odysseus, great glory of the Achaians, and stay your ship, so that you can listen here to our singing..." (The Sirens)

The Odyssey

Homer

Chapter One—Nike

Dusty Souvenir

Dauphin Island had more than its share of weirdness—a fact illustrated by tomorrow's Mullet Toss—but it was home to me. It wasn't as popular as nearby Sand Island or Frenchman Bay, and we islanders clung to our small-town identity like it was a badge of honor. Almost unanimously, islanders refused to succumb to the pressure of beach developers and big-city politicians who occasionally visited our pristine stretches of sand with dollar signs in their eyes. No matter how they sweet-talked the town elders, they left unsatisfied time and time again, with the exception of a lone tower of condominiums that stood awkwardly in the center of the island.

As someone said recently at our monthly town meeting, "We don't need all that hoopla."

That seemed to be the general sense of things, and although I valued what they were trying to preserve, I didn't always agree with my fellow business owners and residents. Still, I was just Nike Augustine, the girl with a weird name and a love for french fries but most notably the granddaughter of the late Jack Augustine, respected one-time mayor of Dauphin Island.

What did I know? I was too young to appreciate the importance of protecting our sheltered island. Or so I had been told. So island folk such as myself made the bulk of our money during spring break and the Deep Sea Fishing Rodeo in July. It was enough to make a girl nuts.

But despite this prime example of narrow-mindedness, I fit in here. Along with all the oddities like the island clock that never worked properly, the abandoned lighthouse that everyone believed was haunted and the fake purple shark that hung outside my grandfather's souvenir shop. I reminded myself of that when the overwhelming desire to wander overtook me, as it threatened to do today and had done most days recently. I had even begun to dream of diving into the ocean and swimming as far down as I could.

Pretty crazy since I feared the water, or more specifically what swam hidden in the darkness. Another Nike eccentricity.

Only my grandfather understood my reluctance, but he was no longer here to tell me I wasn't crazy. My fear of water separated me from my friends, who practically lived in or on the waters of the Gulf of Mexico or the Mobile Bay most of the year.

Meandering down the aisles of the souvenir shop, I stopped occasionally to turn a glass dolphin and rearrange a few baskets of dusty shells. I halfheartedly slapped the shelves with my dust rag and glanced at the clock again and again until finally the shark-tooth-tipped hands hit five o'clock. With a bored sigh, I walked to the door, turned the sign to Closed and flicked off the neon sign that glowed: "Shipwreck Souvenirs." I'd keep longer hours when spring break began, but for now it was 9 to 5.

I walked to the storeroom to retrieve the straw broom. I had to pay homage to tradition and make a quick pass over the chipped floor. I'd had barely any traffic today, just a few landlubbers hoping to avoid the spring breakers; as many early birds had discovered, the cold Gulf waters weren't warm enough to frolic in yet. Probably fewer than a dozen people had darkened my door today, and only half of those had the courtesy to buy something. With another sigh, I remembered the annoying child who had rubbed his sticky hands all over the inflatables before announcing to the world that he had to pee. I thanked my Lucky

Stars that I didn't have kids. But then again, I would need a boyfriend or husband for that, right?

Oh, yeah. I get to clean the toilets, too.

I wondered what the little miscreant had left behind for me in the tiny bathroom. No sense in griping about it. It was me or no one. I wouldn't be hiring any help anytime soon. I grabbed the broom and turned to take care of the task at hand when I heard a suspicious sound that made me pause.

Someone was near the back door, rattling through the garbage cans. I could hear the metal lid banging on the ground. Might be a cat or dog, but it might also be Dauphin Island's latest homeless resident. We had a few, but this lost soul tugged at my heartstrings. I had never seen a woman without a place to live. So far she had refused to tell me her name or speak to me at all. Perhaps she was hard of hearing too? Whatever the case, it sounded as if she weren't above digging through my trash cans. Which meant even more work for me. "Hey," I called through the door, hoping to stop her before she destroyed it.

I had remembered her today as I was eating my lunch. I saved her half of my club sandwich. I had hoped I could tempt her to talk to me, but as if she knew what I had planned, she'd made herself scarce. Until now.

I slung the door open, and the blinds crashed into the mauve-painted wall. Nobody was there, but a torn bag of trash lay on the ground. I yelled in the direction of the cans, "Hey! You don't have to tear up the garbage! I have food for you. Are you hungry?"

I might as well have been talking to the dolphins that splashed offshore. Nobody answered me. "I know you're there! I just heard you in my trash. Come out, lady. I won't hurt you." Still nobody answered. I heard a sound like a low growl coming from the side of my store.

What the heck was that?

Immediately I felt my adrenaline surge. Danger stalked close. I ran to the back wall of my shop and flattened myself against the rough wood. I heard the growl again. Was that a possum? Gator? Rabies-crazed homeless lady? I knew I shouldn't have started binge-watching *The Walking Dead* this week. There was absolutely nothing wrong with my imagination. My mind reeled with the possibilities. After a few seconds I quietly reasoned with myself. I didn't have time for this. Time to face the beast—whatever it might be.

Gripping the broom as if it were a weapon, I tiptoed to the corner of the building and spun around the edge with my broom raised above my head. I shouted, "Ha!" as if that would help me seem more menacing, but to my surprise there was nobody there. Not a scary possum, no alligators and no sign of the zombie homeless lady. Nobody was there but Mr. Targetti, the man who owned the bike rental shop next door. He caught me and snorted in amusement.

"Oh, hi, Mr. Targetti. I thought I heard someone back here. Got into my garbage again." He just stared at me, as he always did. I don't think he'd ever spoken to me. That bothered me. I was a likeable gal. I gave up trying to explain why I'd been brandishing my broom like a katana. I lowered it with a sheepish expression. He raised his shiny black eyebrows even higher, so they looked like they might slip up and over the top of his head. I let out a nervous laugh at the sight. With a grunt of disgust, he turned his broad back to me and headed back inside, all the while shaking his overly large head as if he couldn't believe what he'd just seen.

"One day, your head's going to fall off," I whispered at his back.

I thought I saw him pause, but he didn't turn around again. He slammed the side door of his shop behind him, and I heard the lock snap in place. How could that giant of a man be afraid of little old me? He must have weighed three hundred pounds—hardly the kind of guy you'd think would rent bicycles, but then again who was I to judge? I just turned twenty-two and barely had a high school diploma.

But I had a bad-ass broom, I thought with a big grin. Proud of myself for at least aggravating Mr. Targetti, I swung the broom like a ninja one last time before heading back into the store. Just then, I screamed.

"Cruise! You scared the heck out of me. What are you doing sneaking up behind a person?"

He laughed as he removed his aviator glasses from his tanned face. "You didn't hear me? I guess you were too busy practicing some Karate Kid moves?"

"Karate Kid? How old are you?"

"Hey, that movie is a classic."

"Kind of like you, huh?" I was very much aware that Cruise was only twenty-five, but I liked reminding him of the age difference between us. It aggravated the crap out of him. And that made me extremely happy. Most days. I grinned up at him and cupped my free hand above my eyes to shield them from the sun. Unlike the one other island police officer, he did not wear shorts, despite the fact that he had terrific legs. I liked seeing him in his blue uniform, but it would be a month of Sundays before I told him so.

"Wow. Way to wound a guy. Do you need help with something, or are you leading a raid on Mr. Targetti's bike shop? If so, you might need a bigger broom."

"That guy. Don't get me started. No, I'm good. Unless you want to help me pick up trash. Something got in the cans again."

"You'll have to make sure you put the lids on good and tight next time."

"Geesh, officer. I never would have thought of that."

We strolled back to the mess and began picking up the empty boxes and paper. Thank goodness there was no food in the bags. That would have been totally disgusting.

"I'm just trying to help, Nike."

I tucked my hair behind my shoulder and glanced at him as he picked up trash with me. I was being a jerk, and he was picking up my garbage. Here he was doing something nice for me, and I was being...well, me.

"Sorry, but I could have sworn I put those lids on good. I made sure of it. I heard something out here, so I came out to see. Hey, have you heard any reports about a homeless lady?"

"Homeless lady? No, but there are quite a few interesting characters over at the Sunset RV Park. Quite a few drunks. I have a feeling I'll have a few late nights this weekend."

"Well, there's this one lady. She's about as big as a minute. I've seen her out here wandering around, along the shore there. Looks like she was scavenging. I was thinking she was looking for food, but maybe she was picking up cans or shells or something."

"She bothering you?"

"No. What bothers me is that she might need something to eat. I can't stand the idea of somebody going hungry."

He tossed the last piece of garbage in the can and pressed the lid down, his toned arms flexing as he made a big show of it. I tried to pretend I hadn't noticed. "You remind me of your grandfather. He couldn't stand to eat by himself. I sure miss him."

We walked back inside and washed our hands in the tiny bathroom. Thankfully the child-criminal had not left any surprises like piles of paper towels or anything gross in the sink. I put the broom back and locked the back door. Cruise walked toward the front door, and I followed him so I could lock it behind him. I still had a handful of change to count. How would I ever keep this place going?

"You never did say why you came by."

"Oh, yeah. It was nothing important. Just wanted to see if you were going to eat tonight." He tossed his hat in his hands and avoided my eyes.

"What? Of course. I eat every night." Then it hit me. He was asking me out. Finally. What brought this on?

"Come on, Nik. You know what I mean."

I leaned my back against the counter as he flipped the lock on the front door to open it. "I'm not sure I do know, Officer Castille. What *could* you mean?"

"Do I have to spell it out?"

Now I was getting ticked. How could he expect an answer if he hadn't even asked me out? "What kind of half-assed question is that? Now ask me right."

"Nike Augustine, will you…"

"Come on now, Cruise. Unless you're asking me to marry you, you don't have to use my last name. How long have we known one another?"

"Um, okay, Miss Bossy. You haven't changed since the first time I met you." I didn't let him meander down Memory Lane; I raised my eyebrows like Targetti had.

He smiled pitifully. "If you haven't got plans and you don't have something in the oven, which I know you don't because you don't cook…." I tilted my head, giving him a warning. He tossed his hat again and smiled at me even bigger. "I thought maybe we'd have a drink or share a meal."

"You thought? Haven't got plans? This isn't getting any better."

"Why are you making this so difficult?"

I walked to the door and opened it wide. Waving my hand to show him the way out I gave him my answer. "Since you didn't really ask me, I can't really answer you." His smile disappeared, and I quickly added, "Come by the house around seven and I'll give you my answer."

He tossed his hat up, caught it and plopped it on his head like he was about to climb on a horse. "And wear something nice!" I called after him as he drove off. I grinned like the possum that I couldn't find earlier. This felt right. I had all but given up on Cruise. Again I half wondered what had happened to inspire him to ask me out.

"Calm down, Nike. He didn't give you a ring," I scolded myself. I went back inside, ready to lock it up, race home and get ready for my long-awaited date. Then I came face to face with the homeless lady. I yelled in surprise, and then everything went black.

Chapter Two—Meri

D*ark Halo*
    Quickly I slipped beneath the water's surface to prevent her gray eyes from spotting me. It was not time yet to reveal my true self—I must wait. The command came from Heliope, but it had proved difficult adhering to her rule. I could barely contain my excitement! Once again the time drew near. Friend would awaken and know me—she would recall our adventures.

No more of this haunting her from the water. No more slipping onto the rocks to peek into the window and watch with disapproval as she did human things like toil and clean. We would be together again—as we had been many times before. The times may have changed, at least for the human world, but this time would be no different. Friend would remember me—I would not be forgotten forever! Not long now, *Thess-uh-lo-nike!*

I never called her that. She was Friend.

That was a good thing since my scales were losing their vibrant blue and purple colors and were falling off at a disturbing rate. Glancing at them now, I moaned at the sight. I needed her companionship. Desperately. A mermaid with no Friend was not much of a mermaid.

And I was too far from home. Too far from Friend. I dove and spun in an ever-tightening circle at the thought of being close to her again. The dolphin pod that traveled off the point spun in celebration with me. They did not understand my joy, but they felt it all the same. They were not stupid animals, and they felt deeply.

Neither was I stupid; however, many of the Higher Order believed all mermaids were simpleminded. Let them believe it. Better for me and for my kind. There were few of us now, very few. Not like before when we swam the Azure Circle. We had filled the oceans, befriending and assisting the other Oceanids and even humans. We were made with the need to serve, but that propensity to care for others had not served us well. Not at all. I moaned again as I recalled the faces of my kin, lost now at the bottom of the ocean.

How I have missed you, Friend! Maybe we would swim home. Home to the warmth, to the white stones and the cozy harbor of sparkling blueness. Maybe. It would be a long swim, but we were strong and there were many places to visit along the way. Yes! I would convince her. We would dive the Arch of Reason, skim along the Bimini Road, explore Archimedes' Tomb where the Blood Crocus grew. If I could find those places still. Yes. It was time to leave this place and these strange waters. Besides, no one came to the Sirens Gate anymore. The days of magic were over, weren't they? I moaned again, remembering a different time.

What was that? A ripple of warning trembled through the water like a knife slicing through flesh. I sensed Danger headed toward me. And toward the one I guarded. Danger greater than the kind that rolled off sharks and other large predators. I swam quickly to a nearby reef—an old shipwreck, the only hiding place in this barren space. There were not many reefs here in these murky waters, but this one would hide me nicely. I kicked my wide tail and dove into the shelter, the sense of Danger increasing with each passing moment. Paddling harder as The Danger drew near, I grabbed the railing of the sunken ship. Another wave of Danger washed over me; this one was so strong it nearly knocked me over.

Water has a sound. It's full of life, full of the heartbeats of living things, but now the water was empty and deceptively quiet. Nothing stirred other than the currents, and they were Neptune's children. They always had a mind and will of their own. They followed no rules.

Ping, ping, ping.

Glancing around me, I saw other creatures hiding. There were none of my kind, and no supernatural beings, but the creatures of the sea sensed The Danger too. This did not bring me comfort. There was no comfort in fear. The ocean emptied as The Danger approached. Small fish, large ones, even minuscule creatures swam, crawled and slithered out of sight.

Ping, ping, ping. The Presence searched for something. But what?

I peered through a wooden slat in the ship as the water shook with the approach of this unknown threat. A very young dolphin jetted past me, confused by the seeking signals. He was too young and helpless to hear his own kind over this new, alarming noise. Yet his family searched for him. I could hear them, feel their concern.

Ping, ping, ping.

I screeched at him to pull him away from Danger, even though I knew doing so would reveal my presence. I stared at him, and my turquoise eyes touched his frightened spirit briefly. That would also reveal my location, but in the moment, I cared not. He turned obediently and swam toward me—and then past me. Yes, here The Danger approached!

It hovered above us, not in the water but poised on the glassy surface. I gasped, and it paused. I squinted to see The Danger but could discern nothing. The being cast a wide shadow over all those beneath it. The shadowy figure blocked the setting sun, making the depths even blacker. The figure left only a halo of darkness, and the fading light behind it made it appear even more frightening.

No boat, no ship, no seacraft. So entranced was I with this new arrival that I forgot the juvenile dolphin. Then he swam to the Down Deep, and I watched him as he made long, fluid strokes with his tail, moving as quietly as he could. Eager to keep him safe, I decided to follow him. It was my nature to do so. I was mermaid-kind after all.

Yes, down further would be better. Away. Away from The Danger. But I could not hide from this forever, and I had to know what this was. Heliope would want to know. And Friend. Awareness washed over me.

Within this shadow was an old danger.

A familiar danger. A bad thing.

Yes, this would be bad.

Chapter Three—Nike

Full Awake

I floated above myself for what seemed like hours. Again I was faced with a choice: dip back inside and live or fade away into the eternal night. I had made this choice before. At least I had one, unlike others of my kind. Some less fortunate than I was never had such choices.

Like humans, I had no way of knowing for sure what lay in the beyond, but it wasn't fear that drove me back into my human body. It was that panicked feeling that I had not completed the thing I had been sent to do. But what was that? With what might be considered a deep breath I focused on my body and fell back into it with an unpleasant slap. As I did, I became aware that I was being shaken not merely from the inside but from the outside as well.

"You in there?"

I let the pain subside before I answered the voice. There was always pain with an Awakening. It began at the shoulders and neck and then flowed out toward my fingertips and toes. After that, my head would pound and my heart would thud like a heavy rock slamming against an unyielding boulder. But the pain and discomfort would dissipate, and I would remember. It was usually quick, but this transition seemed off somehow.

Squinting to adjust to my surroundings, I heard her voice again. Low and soft, like my mother's voice, but she was not my mother. "Can you hear me?"

"Yes. I can hear you," I said without moving my lips.

"Good. I thought maybe you weren't all there yet."

"I'm not." I struggled to sit up. I could not move or open my eyes. I struggled to remember her name. My name. I knew that I knew her name, but it escaped my memory. Yet here I was. In my own beach house, in my lumpy bed, as I had been this morning.

I breathed in deeply, trying to embrace my human form again. Yes, I should focus on my surroundings. The smell of honeysuckle candles on my nightstand. The ticking of the mermaid clock on my blue dresser. The subtle smell of fresh paint. I recently painted this room and the wooden headboard of this bed.

Yes, that I remembered, but I couldn't remember who I was. Who she was. What I was doing. Something was wrong. As the feeling of wrongness increased, anxiety stretched me, making me feel as if I would snap in half and be lost forever. What the hell was going on? I felt agitated—anger festered inside me. But at who or what, I could not say. All I wanted was to be left alone to figure this out. To figure it all out.

"Enough of this. How do you want to do this? The easy way or the hard way?"

That she could hear me think made me angry too. I answered without considering my decision. "The hard way!" I growled at her. With a sigh she whacked me on the forehead with the palm of her hand. Then the lamp light faded and I remembered her name.

"Heliope!"

"Mm... hum..."

I don't know how long I lay there like a fever-stricken child, but when I woke up she was still there beside me on the bed, reading a newspaper, wearing a pair of gold-rimmed glasses on a gold chain. I glanced at the clock. It was 6:30 now. Great. I'd been asleep for at least an hour. Maybe more.

I clutched my stomach as the queasiness rose. Another side effect of the Awakening. It was like having butterflies in your stomach times a thousand. The longer the slumber, the more intense the Awakening experience. I should have known this by now. I had experienced this dozens of times, more like a hundred, and it was always the same. But I had no choice. It was sleep a while or go mad.

I scooted up on the bed and leaned against the pillow. Heliope didn't offer to help me, and I did not ask for it. At least we were civil to one another. That had not always been the case. Tossing the newspaper on the rickety nightstand, she handed me a glass of water. It wasn't just any water. Two blue drops of light bounced around in it.

I held the glass, studying the light for a moment. Here I was at this moment again. I had a choice, didn't I? I was awake, but I had not put my immortal mantle back on yet.

It wasn't too late to abandon the supernatural life. Not too late to take my place in the stars.

"You do this every time. Will you please just drink it without all the theatrics? So human sometimes."

I ignored her sarcasm and drank the water. "My brother?"

"Nothing. Not yet."

Suddenly Heliope shed her homeless attire and in a brilliant flash of light, I could see the real her. How could I have thought the great Heliope was mortal? How stupid I had become!

"The glasses were a nice effect. You should wear them more often," I said with a return volley of the sarcastic.

"Did you like that?" She grinned mischievously.

"Yep. Almost as good as my fish tattoo. See?" I turned my left leg to show off the colorful artwork that human me had paid for last month, but the thing was now gone. Nothing remained of that experience but smooth skin. "Oh heck, I wasted seventy-five bucks."

"Well, if it means that much to you, I can put it back."

I glanced at her suspiciously. Heliope's magic had never been reliable. She might actually change me into a fish. "I'll pass. Thanks."

I could see her disappointment, but I wasn't willing to allow her to practice on me. She wasn't a natural.

"Are you all there? I know the process is slow for some."

Yes, I was me again—Thessalonike of Macedonia.

Or what was left of me. I nodded, and the acknowledgment weighed on me like a heavy yoke.

Heliope took my glass and allowed me to stare at my hands for a few seconds. I could see the subtle glistening around my skin. It would fade soon; the purple aura would diminish, and I would appear human to all but the supernatural creatures who might cautiously cross my path. I was the Guardian of the Sirens Gate. The Keeper of the portal to a forgotten world. None of that mattered to me at the moment. The desire to swim and sing nearly knocked the wind out of me. It took every inch of my determination not to slap her out of the way and run for the ocean.

"Slapping me would be a very bad idea," she said, somewhat amused at the prospect.

"Get out of my head, Heliope," I warned her.

"Then close the door, Thessalonike. I am having too much fun in here. Oh, there's a nice memory."

I pushed back against her mental invasion and became aware of her focus. That was my memory she was tinkering with. Memories of Jack and me. Jack washing the dog, Springer. Jack. No. It was too painful to recall right now. I wasn't ready for that. She politely departed my mind. With a nod, she smiled with what might be considered an understanding expression. If you didn't know her as I did.

Her laughter surprised me. Now that I remembered the truth, everything about her seemed supernatural. Her light brown hair glistened with warm light that cascaded through her curls. If I looked closely, I could see an invisible crown of light atop her head, but she wore no jewelry and dressed rather plainly in a light brown dress. "Yes, it's easier to dress plainly. Easier to blend in on this godforsaken island. What was the Order thinking sending you here?"

"I want to swim."

"I know."

"I have missed the water. How long this time?"

"Mmm...about fifty years."

The truth hit me like a ton of bricks, a human expression that worked beautifully now. "Oh no...Jack is gone." It wasn't a question, and I did not require her comment. Jack had been my husband. Many on this island believed him to be my grandfather, but I had cared for him, until I forgot even that. And he knew the truth and had loved me enough to protect me. He kept my secret even when I didn't know it myself. I wondered why. How hard it must have been for him.

Jack!

"He was a good man, but you really had no choice and he made his."

"Tell me what happened. That part is hard to recall, and I don't want to wait." I flicked away a tear with my finger.

"Very well, but there is a man in the driveway. You don't waste any time, do you? He is tall, with nice shoulders, silky brown hair and expressive brown eyes. He reminds me of someone, but who?"

"Oh no! It's my friend, Cruise. We had a date!" *Oh no! I would have to say goodbye to him now.* I couldn't believe the heartache I was experiencing, losing Jack and Cruise in one day.

"See? You sirens are too beautiful and lusty for your own good. Maybe you should tone it down some," she said in an amused lilt. She walked to the window and peeped out through the cheap blue curtain.

"Get away from there, or he will see you."

"I don't care. Let him see me."

I paced the room wringing my hands. I couldn't worry about Cruise right now. To make matters worse, I had a growing need to get back into the water. Meri! I had to see her!

I ran to her side. "You have to get rid of him, Heliope. Tell him I'm sick. Tell him I left to go somewhere or something. Just give me some time."

"Me? I'm not your servant, Thessalonike." She snatched her arm away. I had offended the once-regal queen and semi-divine goddess. She was neither now, but in pride, nothing much had changed. I could almost hear her thoughts: *I do not serve you.*

Why was she being so unreasonable? I would have helped her if she needed me.

"Fine, but you owe me a favor. And I won't forget it," she said as Cruise knocked on the door.

This I knew well. Heliope forgot nothing. Ever. Even conversations from centuries ago she recalled with perfect clarity. "Yes, I know. Thank you." I scrambled to escape the house, the urge to swim overwhelming my desire for Cruise. Maybe it was best to leave it this way.

Or maybe I would make it up to him later, but for now, I had to go where I belonged.

Chapter Four—Heliope

*E**nchanting Shadow***

How on earth did this happen? More than a few hundred years into this relationship, and I was still answering doors for Thessalonike. So this was my punishment? Play house mother to an eternal teenager?

This was not the future I envisioned when I first perched on the gilded couches of Olympus and accepted the cup from the hand of Dionysus. But I owed a debt that must be paid. No matter how menial the task.

I once heard a wise man say that both fresh and salt water cannot flow from the same stream, but I continued to disagree with his observation. For I both loved and hated my charge, but that was no reflection on her; it was the nature of a fallen goddess, which I was now. My divine lover persuaded me to abandon my humanity to be with him. Of course, then he abandoned me...leaving me fallen and him doing who knows what.

I heard the back door slam behind me and knew she had escaped to the water. Let her swim. If I was here, there was a reason and she would need all her strength.

In another time, another place, I would barely be aware of the Sirens Gate or any other gate for that matter. I would rule over kingdoms, lending my wisdom and strength, in return for a fair amount of well-earned worship, of course. How I longed to rule again! It seemed impossible to conceive in this age of independent thinking. How I longed for the past!

Would anyone believe that once I had counseled Queen Boudica of the Iceni? I had come so close to taking all of Britain from the Romans, but I had been betrayed. And my betrayer had been a man. Naturally. Later I became the Grand Dame of Tavistock, and what fun I had then, although it had been nothing like being queen. I laid my hand upon other minor kingdoms and had my share of achievements, but nothing recent and nothing compared to the days when I was Olympias, wife of Philip and Queen of the Civilized World.

I snatched a green apple out of a glass bowl on the kitchen table before walking to the front door. This was a pitiful place. Too cramped and full of human smells. I sniffed the apple. This. Now this smelled like love. It was a wonder that I should want to taste it again. I took a bite and savored the sweet juicy meat. Ah, my sense of taste had not faded. Not at all. The flavor triggered pleasant memories, but I continued my trek to the door. I tried not to dwell on the fact that I, the great Heliope, was again relegated to my least favorite role—stepmother and apparent housemaid. I did not hide my disdain for my task as I opened the door. I did not wait for him to knock.

"Yes?"

He paused, and his bouquet of wilted white flowers shook in surprise at my welcome. A shower of petals fell to the ground. It served him right—that was a pitiful offering. Even for my stepdaughter.

"Excuse me, I am here to see Nik. I'm Cruise Castille. Officer Cruise Castille."

"Well, Officer Cruise Castille. *Nik* is not here. She told me to give you a message. Are you ready for the message?"

"Nik Augustine?"

"Who else lives here? Are you ready for her message?" This one was so handsome but ridiculously slow.

He stammered, "Um, yes?"

"Is that a question? You don't seem sure."

"No, I mean what is her message?" As he put his hand on his hip, more flower petals fell.

"She says she will see you tomorrow and explain everything to you then." I took another bite of my apple and stared at the human man. That wasn't much of a message, but it was the best I could do for now. I wasn't in the mood to be creative. This one was tall—not as tall as a demi-god, but certainly tall for a human.

Demi-gods were at least a head taller than a human, and they had not walked the earth in centuries. Except in some remote places, and those tended to be stark-raving mad. The male specimen before me had long, muscular arms that he showed off with a tight short-sleeved shirt. He wore entirely too much cologne, but I could detect an attractive natural scent beneath the layers of the cheap fragrance.

I leaned against the doorframe and watched him process the information. Officer Castille was nowhere near the most handsome man I had ever seen, but then again, I had lived for a few thousand years; handsome faces were a dime a dozen, as they say. I could tell my scrutiny made him nervous. I smiled, not at him but at my own power. It was nice to see I had influence over someone. Even if it was merely enough to make him uncomfortable. I felt a sudden rush of pity for him.

"And who are you? If I may ask?" His question was courteous enough, but he clearly didn't trust me. I didn't blame him. I didn't trust me either.

I tossed the remnant of the apple into the yard. It landed with a thud near a neglected rose bush.

"You may. I am Nike's Aunt Helen."

"Jack's sister?"

"Hardly." How dare this man think me to be a grandmother? I would have to work on my glamor magic. I could not stomach the idea of spending a moment as an old woman. "No, not related to Jack. Look, it is complicated. Is there anything else I can do for you? I am sure Thessalonike would be here if she could, but she's not. So, goodbye, Officer Cruise Castille." Slamming the door in his face would be very satisfying. However, I had instructions to be polite and blend in. Blend in. As if that were possible on this inbred island.

"Thessalonike. I've never heard her called that."

He didn't quite believe me yet. I could tell by the tilt of his head and the stiff stance he had taken. This whole exchange grew tiresome; I had other things to do, like report the girl's Awakening to the Order. They would want to know about her status, and if I cared about my future, I would be the first to report it. Time to end this exchange. Since Thessalonike cared about this Castille person, I decided the conversation should end with a smile and no blood.

"Oh? You don't even know her name?"

He blushed at the implication. "Nike or Nik. I've known her since school."

"That's nice. Well, whatever you call her, her name is Thessalonike. I will tell her that I gave you the message. Thank you." I went to close the door, but the young man moved quickly and rudely stuck his foot in the doorway. I clenched the door handle, tempted to break the thing into pieces and beat him with it.

"Are you sure everything is okay in there? I have never heard of you. Nik, I mean, Thessalonike has never mentioned you before. She's my friend, and I'm worried about her; I am sure you understand that." He pushed against the door with his hand, but not too far. *Good. Good human. Now go away.* I attempted to speak to his mind, but it was closed. As most humans' minds were.

"I do understand, Cruise Castille," I purred persuasively, "but there is nothing else I can tell you right now. I probably should not tell you this, but there is a private family matter she has to attend to. Come back in the morning for tea. The three of us will catch up then." I closed the door and stood behind it shaking my head. He was a stubborn one.

If she thought she would get rid of him easily, she had another thing coming. Some men were like that. All bossy and pushy. If he were mine, I would put him in his place quickly. I made the mistake of letting a man take the lead when I was young, and it cost me everything. Never again. I would warn her about him, but what she did with him would be her own business.

I heard the gravel pop under the car tires. He took his time leaving, but in the end, leave he did. I smiled and wiped my hands as if I were ridding them of unwanted crumbs. It was one of my favorite human actions. It had been so hard to remember simple things like that when I had last awakened. How long ago had that been now? Twenty years? Twenty-five? Fifty? I had taken only a brief slumber, and the Order had given it begrudgingly. I think they would have been just as happy to see me go absolutely crazy. Maybe I would. Wouldn't that be a fitting end for an unfaithful queen?

Hmm...that was an interesting and troubling development. The Awakening had been difficult for Thessalonike too. I wondered why and made a mental note to investigate. What could it mean?

I made my way back into the bedroom. The girl (to think I still thought of her as such) had vanished; the window was open, but I didn't believe that was her port of departure. I walked to the window and looked out. The sun had disappeared, but I could see clearly even in the darkest night. I could see as well as any owl. I glanced at the sand and could see her footprints. Yes, she was headed to the water.

I heard a dreadful sound. I shed my human exterior; feathers covered me, and I perched on the open windowsill. With my expert owl eyes I scanned the dunes behind the small house. At first I saw nothing. I kept still, not moving a muscle. I could wait. I would wait. As long as it took. I smiled a birdlike smile. I was good at waiting.

Down the beach about a half mile a drunken couple were making love in the sand. A little further dozens of crabs scoured the flesh of a discarded fish. A mouse skittered across the sand. Like a hot flame, my own needs began to burn. FOOD. HUNT. STALK. I did not succumb to temptation, though it took much determination.

Then I saw the thing. A shadow slipped behind the pyramid-shaped dune. It had no discernible figure, but I could see it was purposeful in its movements. This was not its true form. It did not want to be detected. It, whatever it was, did not want to be seen. But I saw it.

Then I heard a splash in the water. The shadow slid across the sand toward the noise.

I watched from a distance and then, when I thought it safe, silently sailed to a scraggly tree between the house and the bay. The shadow spun and folded in on itself.

No longer a shadow. I could see it now.

Harpy!

With bird legs covered in black feathers, the creature's torso was partially covered in black fur, but its breasts were exposed. It swung its head—the head of a woman—around, sensing the surveillance but unable to detect the source. Harpies were stupid but vicious, and its presence disturbed me.

As it let out a birdlike cackle and swung its head from side to side, the creature's greasy hair hung damply around its gnarled shoulders. Standing now on its taloned feet, it stood tall and stared at the water with deadly focus. I followed its gaze. I saw no one, and I was sure that Thessalonike had gone deep into the water by now. The harpy could not swim, and the girl would be in the water for hours.

HARPY! I said, hoping to confuse the animal. I SEE YOU, HARPY!

It spun about with a growl, and its talons dug deep in the sand. It opened its wings threateningly but still could not locate me. If I had been wearing human skin, I would have smiled at that.

GO NOW, HARPY! OR DIE!

The harpy screeched at the threat and walked backwards from the dune. It sensed the direction of my voice but was still too stupid and blind to see me. I would have to make it easy for the creature. I flew from the tree and landed on the sand between us.

I did not return to my human form. Instead I increased my size, confident that this would intimidate the harpy. It screeched again this time; it understood who I was and that I protected Thessalonike. It backed away, nearly tripping over its clumsy wings.

GO NOW AND TELL YOUR MISTRESS WHAT YOU HAVE SEEN!

I screamed in its head. Uncontrollably it began to shake, and in a few seconds it flew away, screeching one last time before departing.

I watched it leave with some satisfaction, but I knew this wasn't the end. Not at all. This was a warning shot. They were surveying the battle ground, acquiring the target. The old battle would continue. Roxana would try again to resurrect Alexander, and for that she would need his sister's blood. It was no coincidence that I was here—she was here, at the Sirens Gate.

I shed my feathers and stood as Heliope now. I glanced up at the stars. "Do you see this?" I asked the Order, pretending to be confident that they could still see, discern and help.

I saw a star sail across the sky and land in the water some distance away. It was so far out that no human would hear it splash, but I heard it. And so would every other supernatural creature on this island.

I hoped it would be enough.

Chapter Five—Cruise

Dangerous Brew

I drove to the end of Chaumont Avenue and parked the car. I had to process what had just happened—and not like a jealous bastard but like a police officer. This wasn't like Nik at all. How could she stand me up? Should I make a report? What would I say?

Hey, I got stood up tonight, and now I want to tell the world. You know, put it in writing.

No thanks.

Aunt Helen? I wracked my brain trying to recall *any* Helen in *any* conversation with Nik and came up with nothing. Now, some woman I had never heard of or seen before was telling me that Nik couldn't make our date because, well, she couldn't give me a reason but gave me some vague message? I didn't know what I expected to accomplish sitting in the car staring at her house with my binoculars, but here I was, being all pitiful. I waited for five minutes, ten minutes, then fifteen.

This was ridiculous. Nik didn't have a car, just a wreck of a bicycle with a faded white basket on the front, so I wouldn't know if she was there or not. I pushed back the unwanted images of Nik tied to a bed screaming for help or lying on the floor of her living room bleeding to death. That was just my vivid imagination. I called her phone, but it went straight to voicemail.

Howdy, and thanks for calling Shipwreck Souvenirs. Take us home with you. Leave a message, and we'll get back to you on our next business day. Thanks!

I stared at the phone but didn't leave a message. She had caller ID, so she'd know I called anyway, and what was there to say?

I rolled down the window, tossed the remnants of the white daisies out and rolled it back up. I saw no movement in the house and only one light was on in Nik's bedroom. I wasn't about to sit here all night like a loser and peep on her. I had better things to do, just as it looked like she did.

To make matters worse, Mrs. Bannister came out of her beach house and tossed scraps to the mangy white cat she was always complaining about. She saw me, and I waved at her. With a snort she pulled her pink robe closer around her, as if I might catch a peek (or want to) and walked back inside. She'd shuffle inside and call the station or call and complain in the morning. I could hear Dan Belloc now: "Peeping on the old ladies now, Castille?"

Dan would love this. The man was an ass, the irritating kind that hung around just to torment me. As if I couldn't handle policing Dauphin Island, population less than a thousand. I could hardly stand working with the old man, but I kept hoping he'd retire. Yes, Mrs. Bannister might not wait to call. She was a complainer, that one. I hoped she complained to me again about those cats now that I knew she fed them. I'd tell her exactly what I thought about her. No, I wouldn't. Who was I kidding? I was too damn nice. That's what Nike always said. I stared at myself in the rearview mirror. Feeling a dangerous mix of rejected and lonely, I cranked the car and drove the short distance to

The Pirateer. Might as well go where I was appreciated. Lucy Patrick would shower me with compliments while she poured me drinks. I knew she wanted me, and she wasn't bad to look at. Better than watching reruns of Cajun Justice or Cops. I'd spent more than a few nights listening to her raspy voice and quirky jokes. She reminded me of a lost movie star, like she didn't belong here at all. Kind of like Nik, but different.

I cruised slowly past Nik's house, determined not to stop, but I did cast a glance in that direction. I saw a figure move in the front window. It looked like Helen, but I couldn't be sure. I toyed with the idea of questioning her further, but what if there was some kind of family tragedy? What kind of jackass would I look like harassing Nik's aunt during a difficult time for their family? I hit the gas and decided to keep to my plan. As I turned my attention to the sand-covered road, a massive black shadow crossed in front of my car and I slammed on the brakes.

What the hell was that? I grabbed the wheel and looked up but saw nothing but a telephone pole with a dim light that had attracted every bug on the island. I couldn't see a thing!

I got out of the car and walked to the front to see if I had hit something. I had felt no impact, but that didn't mean anything. Nope. Nothing. Probably one of Mrs. Bannister's damn cats. That didn't make sense, though, because the shadow had been over the car, not under it. I rubbed my hand through my hair. The hair on my arm stood on end like it did when you were charged with static electricity. To make matters worse, it sure felt like someone was watching me. I looked up and down Chaumont. Most of these houses were rentals, empty until next week and beyond when the spring breakers invaded the island.

"Someone there?" I called into the night.

Nobody answered, but I heard a door close. The blinds on the front door of Nik's shook. Someone had been there, watching me. That's it. I had to check on Aunt Helen, right? I tapped on the door and rubbed my chin.

She opened the door, and her deep green eyes pierced me. "Yes?"

I stuttered under the power of her gaze. "Is everything okay? I think an animal ran out in front of my car from this direction, but I can't be sure."

She grinned at me. For some reason I was reminded of a cat playing with a mouse just before she killed it. "You aren't sure about a lot of things, are you, Officer Cruise Castille?"

"Please call me Cruise, ma'am."

"Ma'am. I can never get used to that." She bit her lip, and it was like a predator looking at a tender meal.

"So you aren't from here, Helen? I thought I detected an accent."

"No, I'm not from here. You say you hit an animal?" She leaned forward and peered at my car. "I don't see anything, and as you can see, I'm in my bathrobe. About to slip in the tub now. Unless you need anything else?" Was she suggesting I come inside?

"Oh, gosh. Sorry. No, I don't need anything at all. I'll see you in the morning for tea, as promised, Helen."

"Great." She gave me an unnaturally wide grin, and that disturbed me even more than seeing the monster shadow over my car. "Good night, Cruise. No more unscheduled visits, all right?"

"Sure, thanks." She slammed the door in my face, and I walked back to my car feeling pretty stupid. Unconcerned with the speed limit, I didn't waste any time getting to The Pirateer. It was easy to spot. Half a pirate ship stuck out over the bay. I sometimes wondered what they'd done with the other side of the ship. I grew up here, went to school at Dauphin Island Elementary, and I'd loved the look of the place long before I was allowed to walk inside it. Now it was like a second home, except for the Augustines' place.

Lucky for me, Lucy was there. "Hey, gorgeous. Gee, you look like you saw a ghost. What's up? If you've got that stomach virus that's going around the island keep it to yourself." She pulled herself back like she wanted to stay far away from me, but her smile let me know it wasn't too serious a concern. As always, Lucy wore cherry red lip gloss, and her soft black hair was short except for flirty bangs that hung in her eyes slightly. She was definitely a beautiful girl, just a bit too sure of herself to suit me. And she wasn't Nik. Or Thessalonike. What a name!

It made sense, though. If she was an Augustine, she could be Greek, right?

"No, nothing like that. Just a change of plans. How about a drink?"

"The usual?" She grabbed a tall glass and filled it with ice.

"Nope. How about putting some booze in it this time? Any kind you like."

Tossing a clean white bar towel over her shoulder, she eyed me suspiciously. "Really? No joke?"

"No joke," I said, settling down on a worn vinyl barstool.

Her blue eyes sparkled. "Oh, baby. Talk dirty to me. I'll hook you up, Cruise. Go ahead and toss your keys in the basket."

I laughed. "What?"

"You know the drill. No driving after drinking, and you'll need to walk home, I promise."

"Great." I pulled out my cell phone and checked for messages. Nothing from the office, and nothing from Nik. Great again. I did as she asked and tossed my car keys in the basket, careful to remove the house keys first.

"What brings you in here on a Friday night? The only reason I'm here is because Mandy has that stomach bug." She shot carbonated soda on top of some kind of liquor, patted a red napkin with a female pirate printed on it in front of me and placed the drink on top of that.

I didn't answer her. "What is this?" I asked.

"I call it Witches Brew. Don't be a wimp. Drink it. Uh oh. Be right back."

I snorted at the name and poked around the drink with the straw. I saw cherries, and the soda looked like cola. I could definitely smell booze. I pierced a cherry with a tiny plastic pirate sword and glanced down at the end of the bar. Two women hovered together talking in low tones. Lucy joined them with drinks, and the three of them whispered for a minute. I'd never seen the other women before, but their shiny black hair made me think maybe they were relatives of Lucy's.

Lucy reminded me of Demi Moore but with a lot more snark. She was pretty, that was for sure, but we'd never had a thing. She made no secret that she was interested in me, but she didn't push it and I liked the way things were. And I wanted Nik, which meant Lucy was definitely off-limits. Those two never got along.

Lucy and I used to play ball together quite a bit as teens, and she always had natural grace, the kind you couldn't learn. She could reach for the ball and catch it almost every time. When she lunged for a volleyball or ran to a base, you thought you were watching a dancer. I was surprised when she dropped out of college during her senior year to work at the Pirateer. Rumor was she gave up a sports scholarship, which seemed like a waste. I could only dream of having such a privilege. My dad had been an island cop, and I followed in his footsteps without question. At least my mother was proud.

I had no idea what she was thinking giving up her scholarship. Lucy wasn't the kind to share her private thoughts. Her mother, Marie, was a piece of work, always drunk. And Marie was a loud, boisterous drunk who commanded attention at all times. Maybe that had something to do with Lucy's dropping out, but she didn't seem to let it bother her. She did her thing and acted like she was happy. Or as happy as she ever was.

Today, she wore a black vest with the Pirateer's trademark red and white striped shorts. Just like the pirates used to wear, I'm sure. I tried not to stare at the way those shorts fit her just right. I couldn't hear what she and the strangers were saying, but it was clear that Lucy was the boss. She slapped the table, and the other two shut up. Made me want to snatch the jukebox cord out of the wall. *Baby Come Back* by Player filled the bar with retro sound.

Appropriate song.

"Sorry about that. Hey, you haven't taken a single sip. Give it a try."

I swirled the icy drink and smiled at her. "Are those cousins of yours?"

"How could you tell?" She smiled as she began to cut up lemons and limes on the white plastic cutting board.

"You guys favor each other. Are they new to the island? I don't remember ever having seen them before."

"I had no idea you were so nosy when you were off duty, Cruise." She smiled and chopped her fruit. "Yes, we're family. They're just here for the weekend, though. I don't think they'd like living here. Not enough mischief to get into."

"Mischief makers, huh? They look harmless enough." I said sarcastically as I glanced at the two women. They tossed back their drinks and walked out a few minutes later. As they passed me, I noted the unusual tattoo on the back of the younger woman's hand, a strange symbol that I knew I wouldn't forget. It was the letter A superimposed over a pyramid and something I couldn't see too clearly. She was shorter than Lucy but had muscular arms, as if she spent quite a bit of time in the gym. I couldn't see much else since she wore jeans and black boots. Her taller friend, cousin, or whoever she was caught me looking and stared back. She was less attractive and had narrow black eyes, a long neck and rough manners. The last part I knew because she paused to let out a long belch before waving goodbye to Lucy. "Didn't stay long. Gone to see Marie, I suppose."

"Stop being a cop, dude. You make my patrons nervous. Hey, grab that case of beer, please. Just slide it up on the counter. Got to stock, just in case." I didn't know what patrons she was speaking of. It was too early for the beach crowd to migrate in yet. Only a few regulars here.

"Sorry, it's a habit. Must be the weekend for families. I met Nik's Aunt Helen tonight too. Lots of visitors on the island this weekend, and it's not even spring break yet." Without being asked, I slid open the beer case and began filling it with domestic bottles.

Lucy stopped her chopping. "Nik's aunt? What are you two now, an official item? 'Bout time, I suppose, since you've been mooning over her since like high school. What did the aunt look like? Do I know her?"

I chose to ignore her snide comment. "I've never seen her before, but that doesn't mean anything. I don't know her family like that. Honestly, I didn't know she had any family left after her grandfather died. So Aunt Helen was a complete surprise. Pretty lady, but she's a bit weird. Speaking of weird, is there a full moon tonight? I saw something weird on the road on the way over."

Lucy put the knife down and stared at me for one hard second. "What do you mean weird?" I noticed that her hand was bleeding.

"Lucy? You're bleeding. Didn't you notice that you cut yourself?"

"Oh, crap." She grabbed a bar towel and pressed on the cut. It was tiny, but it was bleeding like she'd been shot. I closed the beer case and went to take a look. "No," she rasped, "I can handle this." She popped her finger in her mouth and sucked it until it stopped bleeding. When it stopped she said, "Tell me what you saw."

Then I realized if I told her what I had seen, I would have to explain why I was hanging out on Chaumont and why I paused in the middle of the road. "Never mind. Like you say, just being a cop, I guess. Anyway, Helen had an accent, but I couldn't place it. Says she's not related to Jack, so I'm thinking she's from Nik's mother's side of the family. Weren't they foreign or something?" I finally took a small sip of the drink and immediately regretted it. I'd have to rush home soon and take an allergy pill. I was probably the only person on the planet allergic to alcoholic drinks to this degree.

"Excuse me a second. Be right back."

Without another word, Lucy walked outside behind her cousins, or whoever they were and left me to break out in a rash by myself. Lloyd Joshua, the island's postmaster, sat on a stool and looked at me with a nervous smile. "I'll have whatever you are having. You've been lucky enough to talk to Lucy. Dream come true for me. She's never so much as smiled at me before. I wonder if today is my lucky day."

"Oh, what the hell," I said as I offered him my drink after replacing the fat red straw with a fresh one. Just for show, I topped it off with soda from the soda gun, and he gave me money. I didn't know what to do with it, so I tucked it in the tips jar. I'd only had one sip, but I could tell I was going to break out into a terrific rash. It wasn't like anyone cared. One sip couldn't kill me, right?

I waited around a minute for Lucy, but she never came back. The two other patrons didn't start a riot. Ray Lott, the current owner of the bar, took care of the customers and wandered down the bar to me. Ray was short and always wore pointy-toed boots, even when it was 100 degrees out. He was quiet and had a record. I knew that because I had to check him out when he reapplied for his liquor license six months ago. He didn't like me none, but it wasn't anything personal. Just doing my job, as I told him then.

"Did you arrest my bartender, Officer Castille?"

"No way, Ray. I think Lucy would kick my ass if I tried. She stepped outside for a minute. Some kind of family trouble, I guess. Listen, I don't know what I'm doing, and one's my limit, Ray. See you around." With a grunt he took my place and ignored me as I grabbed my keys from the basket and walked outside. No one was in the parking lot. Lucy's old white convertible was gone. Must have been a real emergency for her to leave like that. Why did I get the feeling that I was the last to know what was going on around here? I considered calling to check on her, but she'd seemed in no mood for my input tonight.

Feeling lightheaded, I tossed the keys in the air and tried to catch them. I missed and decided to walk home instead of taking the car. I'd had only a sip, but why take a chance. It was a weird night. All I needed was for Belloc to see me swerve just once. He'd take my badge in a heartbeat. I wondered how I'd even gotten the job to begin with. The guy hated me.

My duplex apartment was only two blocks away, an easy walk on a quiet island. I locked my car up and slid the keys in my pocket. The skin on my neck and arms began to itch from the alcohol—or something. I felt sure by the time I made it home I'd be more clearheaded.

Might as well call it a night. Or that's what I thought when I opened the door of my apartment.

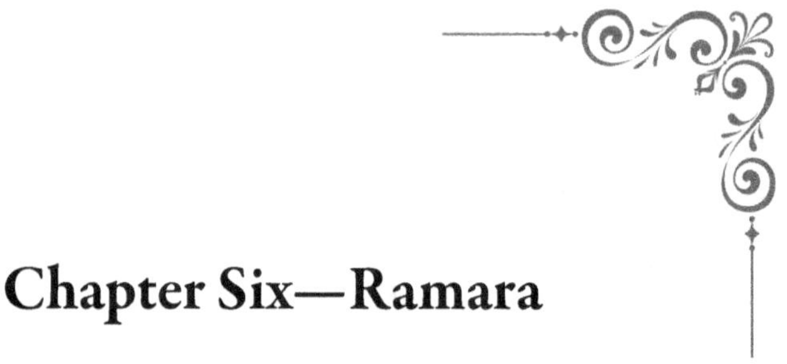

Chapter Six—Ramara

Blue Wings

B I always felt empty when I left the presence of one who belonged to the Order, and today was no different. Faydra's dark eyes bored into mine searching for hidden things, things I wanted to keep from even myself, before she sent me on my way. Funny place to meet, in a jail cell. Perhaps she was trying to remind me that I was her prisoner or nothing more than a slave of the Order.

Who knew, really? Who could understand the ways of the Order? Were we all their slaves?

Those weren't really Faydra's eyes, but rather the eyes of a weak-minded vessel who had the misfortune of being in the wrong place at the wrong time. I shivered knowing that Faydra's power would leave the human and take her memory of the event—and maybe her life—with it. It was always that way, but that was not my concern, I reminded myself. Visits from the Order were rare, and when they occurred one had a duty to obey. Or face the consequences. I had been summoned, and I would answer the call.

"Winged One, took you long enough. Must be getting too old to fly."

"Not too old to perform my task and receive my reward. What is it you request, Faydra?"

She chuckled, low and cold. "Always the mercenary, Ramara. I knew you were the one for this."

I waited patiently for the details. Then I heard something I had not heard in my entire existence. I heard Faydra cough. She coughed and growled as if she were struggling for control of the borrowed body. I didn't offer to help her. Eventually she continued her instructions. "Roxana has landed on these shores. She has the bones and no doubt has found the Sirens Gate—the last portal into the supernatural world."

"She'll need blood, then. Is that why you summoned me?"

Faydra didn't offer any clues. She either didn't know or didn't want to divulge what she knew. She continued, "Roxana's powers have grown. Thessalonike has awakened but is still weak. She will need your protection for a little while. The bigger concern is the gate.

You must keep Roxana from it at any cost." Faydra's human host whimpered in protest of the intrusion into her body and mind, but Faydra soon regained control and continued her speech. Her voice sounded as strong as ever, but the words flowed together in a hard-to-decipher stream. I tried not to grin. The human she had selected was stronger than Faydra believed. How amusing that she would make such a miscalculation!

"What is my reward?"

"You shall have another hundred years."

"Is that all?" I frowned at her. I grew weary of life. Eternity seemed a poor reward for someone destined to remain alone.

"What is it you want, then? You cannot have what it is you seek."

My hands on my hips, I peered down at the dark-skinned woman with Faydra's eyes. "I want my revenge."

"Nemesis has been punished, Winged One. Her sentence is not yet complete. What you ask is impossible."

"Impossible? For the Order?" I snorted derisively. "Hardly, lady. I want my revenge."

"Such a human response, Ramara. This is beneath you."

I jutted out my chin. "You can stop the name-calling. I at least want to *see* that she is being punished."

Faydra began to cackle, and the woman's body rocked back and forth. "Very well. Perform your task, and I shall grant you what you ask. You will be permitted to view her, but you shall not speak to her or approach her." I nodded in agreement. My blood raced at the thought of seeing Nemesis in chains. "This is an untried gate, Ramara. It has never been breached. Assess the gate and protect the girl, but remember the gate is more precious than anything. It is the last one of its kind."

"Yes, Faydra. I will keep them both intact."

"You will. And remember, Alexander's sister is not for you." She coughed and tried to add something to her command, but I could not make it out. Something about "not permitted," and I had a pretty good idea what she was talking about.

Happy that I had managed to get what I wanted, I accepted my assignment and walked out of the jail. Under the protection of the Order, nobody much noticed me. "Remember your oath, Ramara," Faydra purred a warning. I paused at the door. The disembodied voice filled my ears, but I did not turn back to see the body Faydra would leave behind. Senseless death nauseated me.

Instead I wondered what Alexander would think about all this. He'd been dead for a millennium or two, yet his wife held on to his bones like he was a pet dog. The man I knew in life would not have wanted that. Alexander had been fierce, but he had been no match for the machinations of his beautiful wife, Roxana. I remained convinced that she had been his total and irrevocable undoing.

Once I envied him his beautiful wife, his illustrious name—and the victories that he held! His name was upon the lips of the world. How quickly it had all been undone. I envied him no more, for I understood the truth—women made men weak. The old warriors believed that too, but the young never listened. I had been a fool, just like Alexander, but I was alive and he was not. It was the weakness of men—and some eloi or angels, as we are sometimes called—to burn for women in spite of the danger.

Staying on course, I walked with purpose toward the bay. I could see the water now. I pulled off my t-shirt and dropped the rag on the ground but left my jeans on.

My wing tattoos on my back and arms tingled as I drew closer to the source of my power. I kicked off my shoes and did not pause at the edge of the Mobile Bay. I dove in and swam deep until I felt my wings expand. Power streamed through my veins, and I soared upward, cutting through the salty water like a beacon of light. Up I flew until I was above the rain-heavy clouds that gathered over the county. At moments like this, I wondered how I could have been so foolish. Why would I want to leave this behind? Yet I had been so willing to do so for Nemesis.

And she had betrayed me.

I growled as I flew faster, as if I could leave my shame and frustration behind. Nemesis was gone now. Unfaithful to the end, she'd cuckolded me with a human whom she summarily tricked into his death. What a fool Narcissus had been, but no bigger fool than I. He was human, after all; I was angel-kind and of greater strength and intelligence. I knew the cost and had been too willing to pay it.

Now I had another chance to prove my commitment to the Order. And I wanted my prize. I wanted to see Nemesis suffering as I had suffered. I would not fail.

Chapter Seven—Nike

Swim Free

S   I hit the water with a thud. It wasn't a graceful dive from the rocky jetty, not by any stretch of the imagination, but it served the purpose. In the water now, I closed my eyes against the saltiness and paddled deeper, deeper, deeper. When I got to the right depth, I waited, hovering there like a lazy water angel. The seconds turned to minutes as I waited. A normal mortal would have been scratching her way to the top of the water by now, gasping and praying for air, but I was no normal woman.

I was a siren, saved from death by Dionysus who saw me fall from the cliff that day and transformed me before I crashed into the water. I had not been human for many years, more years than I cared to calculate.

At least I was sane.

Some sirens refused to slumber, and sleep was crucial to stop the madness of loneliness from overtaking our minds. Mad sirens could become creatures called rages, like the fabled Lorelei who dwelt to this day in the Rhine River and was a threat to the anonymity of the Order. Luckily for Lorelei, there was no one yet strong enough to remove her from where she was trapped under the Rock of Dancing. I shuddered at her fate. I did not know her, but she had once been a mortal woman, just as I had been. As all sirens had been. We were not what men called demi-gods or gods. Not at all. But by some magic we had become supernatural beings.

These were the thoughts that filled my mind as the complete Awakening occurred. I had been asleep, happy to stumble through a mortal life, forgetting who I truly was and what had happened to me. That time had ended. Now my secret self had forced me to remember, and that could only mean one thing. Danger was close, danger to me. I had to learn what or who the danger was and quickly. For now, I still hung in the water unmoving, waiting for the complete change. Unraveling the memories, I recalled the truth slowly at first; then it began to unwind faster and faster.

I was Thessalonike—daughter of King Philip of Macedonia and sister of Alexander the Great.

My brother always liked that name, Alexander the Great. Unlike some of the heroes of old, my brother was not a humble man but confident and at times even impudent. But he was also the bravest, strongest man I had ever known. He encouraged the name Great. He believed it—as had we all at one time. I could almost hear the adoring crowds ringing in my ears now as I recalled the day I walked the promenade and watched him take the city of Heliopolis: "Golden Alexander! The Conqueror of the World! May he live forever!"

The sound had drawn attention to my brother, attention he had not expected. For he would indeed be offered a chance to live forever, so impressed were the Secret Ones of the Order who watched. He would be offered the Immortal Waters—if he could retrieve them. He would find them, he pledged, and when he did—everything changed. The memories faded as my body began to tremble.

As the waters strengthened me, the power of the rebirth was so strong that it spun me in the water like a tiny top. Water rushed around me, and when I dared to open my eyes, I could see a faint glow of amber light surrounding me. I heard the thinnest whisper of a song. It wrapped around me like a living thing and sent sparks falling down around me. Here was the evidence of my power. My hair spun above me, and I was ready to release my last human breath.

At least until I fell asleep again. This sleep had done me good. I no longer felt the creeping madness at the borders of my mind. The weight of a hundred lifetimes before this one did not weigh me down anymore. I remembered the faces of the men I had loved, the children I had during my first life, and did not want to scream.

I was calm now. All was calm.

I released the last of the oxygen, and here was the test. If the Order accepted me, if they approved my Awakening, I would live. If they did not, this would be the end of me. With a slight tinge of fear, I released my breath into the water and took the sea into my lungs. At first, I felt the stinging pain, but then it subsided as my gills appeared under my arms. I had passed the test. The Order still wanted me. The knowledge exhilarated me, and I dove deeper now that I could easily handle the water pressure. I did not have the fins of a mermaid, but I had very powerful legs and hands.

I began to sing an old song, one all sirens know intuitively. I sang it loudly but under the water so no man would be harmed for the hearing. That was in my power too. A mermaid's power was in her tail, in her great beauty. A siren's power was in her voice and her captivating eyes. I thought of nothing and no one as I swam up now and prepared to breach the surface that waited high above me. I kicked my feet once, then again when suddenly a pale face appeared before me.

Meri!

Her frightened appearance surprised me because I had been so intent on breaking the water, just once! I needed to feel the ocean pass over my body. She shook her head and grabbed my foot, pulling me down to a shipwreck that I just noticed. I tried to pull away, for the excitement of the breach was too great, but she would not relent.

Before I could scold her, she pointed to the surface and sent a wave of fear toward me. She could not speak, not on land or on the water, but she was adept at sharing her feelings. So intense was the fear that I could not ignore her pleading. Obediently, I took her hand and joined her in the shipwreck. I scanned the area for unusual sounds or songs but heard nothing. Whatever it was waiting for us up top, it was not siren-kind. I gave her a questioning look. She shook her head and made a motion with her fingers. A familiar motion. I had seen her use it before and could almost remember it. But what was it?

Fear, fear, fear, her waves of emotion hit me again one after another.

They slapped me, and I waved at her to stop. *I understood what you meant the first time, Meri. Stop that.*

She smiled at me and hugged me lovingly, and her short blond hair poked out around her triangular face. Without realizing it, she sent me waves of love again. I let them roll through me without making a fuss. If there were some supernatural creature stalking us, it would be easy for it to find us if Meri continued to be so free with her feelings. I patted her to remind her to be still. We hovered there side by side, waiting to see what was above.

Then I saw what she saw, what she pointed up to with her glowing white hand. I could tell by the slight bulge in her wide turquoise eyes that she needed air, but I had no oxygen to give her. She would die rather than give away my location. I could not have that on my conscience.

I grabbed her hand and swam using my fast feet to remove us from the immediate danger. I swam for the outcropping behind the old fort. There were plenty of places to hide there. I shoved her to the top of the water, and she whooshed up quietly and took in the air she needed. She must have been below for some time, for mermaids needed air only every few hours. Intuitively she kept herself out of the moonlight, for she would glow brighter under the light of the moon. In the half light, I could see Meri's scales—they certainly looked the worse for wear. I had been gone too long. Mermaids didn't have owners; they weren't pets, as some thought. I've heard mermaids referred to as "the dogs of the sea," but Meri was not a pet—she was a true-blue friend.

I liked that human phrase: true-blue. That was an apt description for Meri from her eyes to the scales of her tail. I needed to heal her, but that would have to wait until the danger passed. The use of healing magic would draw the attention of any supernatural creature. I closed my eyes and pushed myself under the water so I could not be seen.

I surreptitiously listened to the activity around me. I could hear Meri's heart beating fast, even for a mermaid. I heard a pair of dolphins in the nearby shipwreck; one was very young, newly born. Not far away were a group of black-finned sharks, curious about our sounds, but they quickly lost interest and left. There were dozens of hermit crabs crunching their knuckles in their shells; they remained hidden in the sands beneath us. Various forms of sea life scratched and stirred, but none wanted to be noticed. Not now. Then I heard something else. This was definitely a supernatural creature because it had a voice. No, two voices!

Suddenly out of nowhere, the sound of a major splash crashed behind me. Whatever it was that had stalked us just moments ago disappeared quickly, frightened by this new arrival.

What did this mean? Were there two of them now?

With some trepidation, I popped my head out of the water just in time to see Ramara emerging shirtless with expansive pale blue wings behind him. He was supernaturally handsome, and for a moment I completely forgot about Cruise. But then I would have to, now wouldn't I? I wasted time thinking about this eloi in such a way. Besides, could I so easily dismiss the attraction between Cruise and my mortal self? It was known that Ramara had taken an oath of celibacy, which he had broken for the goddess Nemesis. He had only recently been accepted back into the Order. Would I really be the one to cost him his wings? Or his life? Still, as I watched him my attraction grew. This was also in my nature, not a remnant of my mortal personality. I had been remarkably shy and not free with my heart as a human. Cassander had beaten that out of me shortly after we married.

Ramara flew over us now, then landed on the rocks and looked around him, his fists clenched. His shoulder-length, wheat-colored hair flew in the night breeze, and he squatted as he scanned the periphery with his excellent sight. Seeing no danger and without saying a word, he reached down and extended a warm-looking hand to me.

"Thank you for coming," I said. "Just a moment. I have to heal Meri."

Excited at my words, Meri sent me at least a dozen of those love-waves until I told her to stop. "I can't do this if you don't stop, Meri." I laughed at her as I swam beside her to the jetty. She slid up on the rocks, smiled at me and put a hand over her mouth as if that would stop her from sharing her feelings. I didn't expect that it would. Mermaids had notoriously short attention spans. Like human children. I reached for a handful of sand and rubbed it in my hands. I whispered healing words and rubbed her scales with the glowing mixture. Immediately they took on their original blue and purple colors, almost iridescent. Meri tilted her head back and raised her hands above her head, her face the picture of perfect happiness. She touched the scales and clapped her hands delightedly. Love waves came toward me, and I accepted them.

"Go swim now, Meri. I must talk with Ramara. All is well." She gave me a questioning look. "Yes, it is safe."

With a happy smile she splashed around, showing off her strong healed tail. She reminded me of a little boy I used to know, one who used to love showing his mother how quickly he could run in his new sandals. "Look, Mama!" I shook my head, refusing to delve deeper into the painful memory. I had just emerged from my sleep; I could not do this now. I climbed up on the rocks and felt my gills begin to fade after the ocean water seeped out of them like two faucets. If the eloi noticed, he did not say anything. He was standing above me now, looking even taller and more handsome. Oh my. It had been a long time since I had made love.

What is wrong with you, Thessalonike? You act as if you have never seen a handsome man before. And he's not even a man!

Trying to sound aloof and official, I asked, "Why have you come, eloi? Has the Order summoned me? Have they changed their minds? I have only just passed my testing." I spoke with a defiance I really didn't feel.

"I have come for you, princess. Faydra sent me. She says that Roxana comes, if she's not already here. She will attempt to open the Sirens Gate. And you know why she has come. I don't doubt it. A rage stalked you. Never seen her before."

"Nobody calls me princess anymore, eloi," I said as I crossed my arms over my chest.

"And most people call me Ramara, not eloi. Does anyone call you siren?" He did not crack a smile, but his voice was warm and deep, and I noticed a peculiar scent coming from his skin. Pheromones. He probably wasn't aware that sirens were very sensitive to them. We were lusty creatures, after all.

"Call me Thessalonike, and I will call you Ramara. Tell me about this rage."

"Black hair, blue magic, not tall, not short. I would like to see where you live so that I can determine how to protect you."

Who could that be? I thought I knew all the rages, or at least their names. "I am not a novice at this, Ramara. I have all the skills and strength I need to guard the gate, or else they would not have left me here. Go tell Faydra that I am well protected and have many allies."

To my complete surprise, he gripped my wrists savagely. I could see perfectly painted wings on his skin where his own wings had been a moment ago. "You do not command me. Now do as I ask."

Meri splashed nearby, and I could feel waves of anger directed at him. I snatched my arms away. "What do you think you are doing, touching me like that? I did not give you permission to touch me!" I snarled at him.

Now he laughed. "Are you sure I shouldn't call you princess? Call off your dog. I won't touch you again."

I stared at him hard, trying to pretend that I did not want to wrap myself around his waist and smell him all night long. I said, "No, if you are coming with me, it's this way. Just a second." I sent Meri a message.

Meri, I have to go with the stupid eloi. He thinks he can protect me. Ha! Stay close. Swim behind the house, and I will come see you as soon as he leaves.

She sent me a wave of love and swam away quietly around the jetty toward my beach shack. I wouldn't have to show her the way. She'd been protecting me the whole time—that I knew. And now this eloi wanted to show up and be my hero? After all these years, I'd had enough of heroes. The supernatural ones always let me down, and my human lovers had other shortcomings. I could only outlive them.

I stomped away from him and walked down the road toward my small beach house. Hopefully he would get lost before we got there. I wasn't sure I could trust myself to be alone with him. And I was angry that the Order would send him without first consulting me. I didn't trust them, whoever they were. I never had.

A car passed by, and I suddenly remembered my date with Cruise. I wondered what Heliope had told him. *Oh no, Heliope!* She had probably destroyed my house by now. She was the messiest "supe" I'd ever met. Once when we stayed together for a short time in Malaga, about three centuries ago now, she'd managed to burn the place down. I jogged quickly down Chaumont Avenue, my soggy tennis shoes popping along the white gravel. The Crazy Cat Lady at the end of the street stared at us from her bedroom window. "Just going for a run, Mrs. Bannister," I said with a wave. *Pay no attention to the shirtless, barefoot man behind me. And don't tell Cruise,* I thought.

"This way," I whispered fiercely at Ramara. We entered the back of the house, and I called for Heliope. I didn't want her to hit us with her clumsy magic by accident. She did not answer, but I found her quickly enough. She was sitting in my bathtub—fully clothed, thankfully—with a ridiculous amount of water and soap bubbles on the floor. She'd drunk both bottles of my wine and was sleeping under the water. Not dead. She couldn't die. But she was under the water nonetheless. Ramara came in behind me and groaned at the sight.

"So this is what a fallen goddess looks like? I'm not impressed."

"Shut your mouth. She's my friend and technically a relative. Now help me get her up and onto the bed. She can't help how she is. She's been a bit upset since she got tossed out of Olympus."

"Move out of the way. I can carry her." He slid his arms into the bubbles and picked Heliope up as if she were a feather. A drunken, soap-covered feather.

"This way. Let's put her in my bed." I flung throw pillows on the floor. "I'll take Jack's old room if I need to rest." I patted Heliope dry with a soft pink towel and tapped on her cheeks for a few seconds, but she did not stir at all.

"Let her sleep it off, Thessalonike. You know how wine affects the gods—she'll be drunk for days, I'm afraid. Unfortunate, since Roxana is here on the island now. That's one fewer ally for us. We'd better talk about a plan."

"So what do you know? I'm sure it's more than I do. I just woke up."

"And how are you doing with that? Do you need anything?" As he spoke, his bronze hand touched his neck, as if he were looking for something. Then I remembered what he'd lost. What Nemesis had stolen from him. A single pearl on a golden thread. It was an ancient source of power that was as rare as it was lovely. At one time, the pearl had given him tremendous power and the ability to completely heal himself or another during extended battles, but it had been taken from him by his lover—a lover who had betrayed him.

"I am sorry about your necklace, Ramara. I am no friend of hers."

He nodded and dropped his hand, looking ashamed that he had been caught reaching for his lost treasure.

I could read his face just as I knew my own mind. The heat from the betrayal was still fresh. And something else was there...he was determined to seek revenge. That was a dangerous place to be. People who sought revenge always made foolish decisions.

I wondered which one of us needed protection more.

Chapter Eight—Roxana

*A*lways Remember

"*Do you hear them, my love? It is your name that is upon their lips! How many thousands have declared you King of the World? It is well known that you are the greatest king who has ever lived. But alas, my warrior-king, this cannot last. Triumphs are forgotten. They carry us for only so long. You must be an Eternal King!*"

"*What do you mean?*"

"*You know what I mean. You have to find and drink the Immortal Waters. You were invited to do so! Then you—and I—will live forever. We will never be apart again, Alexander. Don't you want that? Wouldn't you like to spend the rest of eternity with me?*" *The golden coins of my dress tinkled like music as they bounced lightly on my hips. A blue stone hung on my forehead. I was a queen and dressed like one.*

He had laughed—not at me, he never laughed at me—but at the idea of living forever. "I know that some men want to live forever, but I look forward to life after this one."

"*You talk like a poet," I said, "Surely you are teasing me, Alexander." I flew out of our bed and stood in front of him as he grinned, his golden hair around him on the pillow like a halo. With his golden skin and hair, he was almost all gold, except for his warm brown eyes. When I first saw him, I knew he would be mine. Even if it had not been arranged, Alexander would be mine.*

Forever mine.

And he did find the Immortal Waters, but it wasn't me he wanted to share those holy waters with.

That honor he wished to bestow upon his sister, Thessalonike. Those two always had an odd connection; I must admit, if only to myself at the time, that I suspected something else lay behind the sister-brother bond. Growing up, they weren't so close that they could not part.

In fact, Alexander barely gave her a second thought until he returned from Egypt full of new ideas about dynasties and bloodlines. He'd consulted the Holy Librarian in the city of Karnak and came to new conclusions about his own destiny. He came home to find his younger sister quite grown up. I quickly arranged her marriage to that awful man, Cassander, and just as instructed, her new husband quickly filled her belly with children. There was nothing my husband could do about the union, not unless he wanted to go to war with one of his closest allies. Three sons, she had. Now they were three long-dead sons. Like my own boy. I blamed her for that. I always would.

I stood in the crow's nest of the lighthouse that overlooked the small barrier island. I sensed the ghost's presence in the tower below me, but I had no fear of it. What could one lingering spirit do to me? Ghosts were usually very stupid. *At least this one has enough sense to get out of my way.*

If anyone had cared to look carefully, they would have seen me. But there was no light shining now, as the moon hid behind a cluster of clouds. I caressed the bag of bones beside me. "No, there is life in you, my love. You will live again." My long dark hair and black gown whipped around me like a shroud. A breeze rose against me. Probably some weak magic sent by the Order. They had become weaker, hadn't they? I had not communicated with them in centuries. Since I no longer slumbered, I did not need to pass their foolish tests. I was strong and nowhere near mad. I no longer observed their traditions and customs. I did not flock to their shores or seek them out. I rejected them completely. I twisted my hair with my fingers as I smiled. This wasn't over yet. I would continue my quest until Alexander and I were reunited—and Thessalonike was dead, dead, dead!

I imagined her warm blood, feeling it flow over my hands—all of it. I fantasized that the last thing she would ever see would be my face. I even knew what words I would say to her. With the help of my new friend, I would have my fantasy. I would open this gate at the appropriate time and greet my husband as he escaped from the Land of the Dead forever. And with the blood of Thessalonike, the gate would have all the power needed to summon not only his soul but the Faithful too. And when that happened, I would pour the Immortal Waters in his mouth and he would live forever.

I sat beside him, rubbing the silk that covered what remained of his bones and skull. Then I lay down beside him and caressed the fabric.

"It's all right now, my love. We are close. This gate is a good one. This is the right one. I can feel it. Your sister will help us; she wants us to be together, Alexander. I know it. I feel it. All is well, my love. You will have your life again. Just as I promised." Tears filled my eyes as I remembered my vow to him. I shut out the memory of his betrayal. He had been coerced into leaving me, taking another wife, abandoning his son and me for Babylon where he died. I chose to remember him as my lover, friend and soul mate. "I forgive you, Alexander."

I ignored the musty scent of the wrappings and the feel of his light bones. How many years had I carried him with me around the world, looking for the Immortal Waters? In life he had refused to share the knowledge with me; it took hundreds of years for me to find them myself. I was nowhere near as clever as Alexander, but I was more determined. Always more determined.

Now here we are together, my husband, under the moon in a strange land far away from our beloved Macedonia. Another island, another gate. We will try again, and we must be victorious! Yes, look, Alexander. Even the stars are on our side. See the bright one there? That is a portent for us, my love. She watches and waits.

A voice behind me called my name: "Roxana!"

I sat up in surprise. "I did not summon you here, Faydra. Why are you here?"

"This is your one warning. Go back to your homeland. You do not belong here. I know what you want. You do not have permission to open the gate."

"I will not leave, and I will have what I came for. Alexander will live again." I added with hatred, "I do not need your permission."

In Faydra's current incarnation, she had dark skin and dark hair. This was not the true her, for I had seen her red hair and green eyes. She had been lovely then, but now she was weak, forced to "borrow" bodies to communicate with her lackeys. *Pitiful.* Now her eyes shone like two pale blue orbs. So empty. So dead. She gave me a crooked smile, further proof she was losing her grip. "Have you forgotten how that turned out the last time? Alexander is too old; he has been dead far too long to come back as he was. This is not his world anymore. He is king no longer. You will not have the man you want," she said as if she knew exactly what she was talking about. I did not trust or believe her.

"Lies," I whispered. "Her blood is all I need. How dare you abandon him now? You, of the Order, sent Alexander to find the Immortal Waters. You would deny him his prize?"

"His destiny is there." She pointed toward the bundle of black silk beside me. "He had his chance to drink those waters with you, and he did not. He saved them for someone else. He chose his path." She smiled. "Do yourself a favor and drain your own blood or go to your Eternal Sleep. It is time to end your miserable life, Roxana. You had no right to drink the waters."

My anger raged, and I lifted my finger to her and watched as the flames leaped from the tip of it. Without a word or a look of fear, she blew them out. "Save your strength, Old Queen. If you insist on pursuing this course of action, you will lose. And you will lose your immortal life."

I laughed, slowly at first, then louder and more raucously. The idea that I could die. How many times had they tried to kill me? How many times had I been cut, drowned, starved and even boiled? Nothing could kill me. Let them drain me! I would live still! All I had to do was endure the pain, and I was quite good at that.

"That is quite a threat, Faydra. Perhaps you are only jealous because you must constantly possess and destroy humans to make your will known to *your* servants. I have the same body I have always had. I am still young, and I look as I always have. That must frustrate you so." I stepped over Alexander and walked toward her. Faydra took a step back, no doubt unsure of what I would do. "Now, now, Faydra. Wouldn't you like to have your own body back? Wouldn't you like to sip the waters? I have hidden them somewhere. I wonder what you would give me in exchange for a drop or two. Maybe a certain Macedonian princess?"

I noticed Faydra lick her lips as if she were actually considering my offer, but she did not ask for the precious waters.

"Leave, Roxana. This is your last warning."

I grew weary of her and no longer feared her. If she could do anything to me, she would have already done it. I lay down beside Alexander and put my arm across the bones. "No more of your warnings, Dying One. Do not get in my way." She vanished, taking her stinking human host with her. So the Order knew I was here, what I intended. Good.

I hated to kill Thessalonike without an audience. This had been a long time coming.

Chapter Nine—Nike

W*alk Home*

We'd barely gotten Heliope halfway dry when the first scroll appeared in the air. I heard the sound first, a slight throb of notes, like an ancient lyre stroked ever so lightly. "Must be for you, princess," Ramara said. I rolled my eyes at him. Would he always call me that? I accepted the scroll from the hand of the invisible delivery man and looked at the seal. "The Order," I said to myself. Of course, who else would it be? I knew nobody else who delivered scrolls via invisible messenger. I pulled the golden silk ribbon and cracked the seal as I unrolled the message.

"What does it say?"

"The Order is happy that you, Thessalonike of Macedonia, have awakened from your most recent rest. Please be aware that Roxana, your sister-in-law, continues her quest and intends to enlist your help in reviving your brother, whether you agree or not. She is on the island and has your brother's bones. Undoubtedly, you will want to resist her, but please be advised that warfare near the Sirens Gate is forbidden. Anonymity is a top priority of the Order. We are sure you understand the need for such precautions. Please know that the Order intends to stay out of this disagreement, and we advise you to keep the fighting to a minimum. It may be best to find ways to amicably agree on some terms that satisfy you both. It is time to end this long feud."

I could not believe what I was reading. Was this a government document or instructions from the Order?

"While we do not support Roxana, we must warn you again: do not put our sanctuary at risk. If you are unable to protect it, you will force us to find a solution of our own. These words are issued by the Order. Heed them."

Shocked by the message, I stared at it a full minute before I crumpled it up into a ball and tossed it on the floor. "What does that mean? If they don't want me to defend myself, why did they send you? Why was I awakened? They could have left me to sleep—Roxana could have killed me as a human, and I would never have known any of this. What is happening with the Order?"

"Something is wrong." He sat on the wooden chair awkwardly, his elbows on his knees. He clapped his hands angrily. "Faydra sent me. She specifically told me to protect the gate and to protect you. But there was something different about the request." My eyes widened as I listened to his warm voice. I pulled my hair over one shoulder and twisted a strand as I sat at my white painted wooden desk, my feet in the chair.

"What do you mean?"

"You are not their number one priority, princess. I don't think they will protect you as they once would have. The Sirens Gate is the last gate. Its value is greater than the threat of a re-emerging Alexander. At least as they see it."

I sat in the chair opposite him staring at the two green apples in the bowl between us. "So I am expendable now?"

"It appears so. This scroll is a warning."

"How could the Order be so weak now? What has happened? I don't know if this is related, but my last Awakening was difficult. Their magic didn't help as it once had. I still cannot recall the details from my last incarnation. I can remember the old lives, but not the most recent ones."

He grunted in agreement. "The human Faydra spoke through struggled against her. It was strange. I have never seen her lose control of a host before. I remember when she did not need one. I hate to say this, but her power has diminished."

"That is odd. I haven't seen Faydra for hundreds of years."

"No one has. She no longer appears to us in her original form. She always uses hosts now, a trick she learned about five hundred years ago."

"Stranger still. Something is wrong." Heliope snorted in her sleep and turned in the bed. "Maybe when our drunken goddess wakes up she can tell us what happened. If she knows."

"I have no use for goddesses, drunken or otherwise." Ramara walked out of the room, rubbing the tattoos on his wrists.

I don't know why, but I followed him out the door. He walked outside, flipping off the back porch light as he did. I liked that. It was completely dark out here, except for one light shining from Targetti's bike shop. I had half a mind to sing a note or two, just enough to burst the bulb, but I'd just been warned, hadn't I? I had to keep my anonymity. The island was cloaked with magic that hid the truth about many of its residents. Most of its residents.

Ah yes, there were many of us here on Dauphin Island. This place had become a refuge for ocean-kind. I began to scan through the people I knew and wondered who was truly who? We were an island of supernatural beings, living peacefully alongside the human residents, but that worked only if the humans believed we were humans too.

But I had no intention of lying down on the stones under the gate and allowing Roxana to slice my wrists and drain my blood. Never!

I watched Ramara stand by the water's edge. I saw him breathe in and breathe out, taking strength from the water. Yes, we were Oceanid creatures. This was who we were. These weren't the waters of our beloved Mediterranean Sea. No, these were darker, wilder and full of strange Gulf Coast creatures. Harmless, for the most part, except for the supernatural creatures that used to call this place home.

Most islanders these days had no idea that Dauphin Island had once been called Massacre Island for a very different reason than the one they taught the local schoolchildren. Not simply because Native Americans had a battle here, but because there had been a civil war between vampires and humans. The humans lost, but the vamps hadn't lived long afterward. We came and vanquished them, claiming the island as our own. We could never allow vampires to guard the Sirens Gate. That would be obscene. We drew exceptional powers from the waters, while that particular band of vamps were air creatures. It had been a tremendous battle—they had the numbers, but we had the strength. At least we did back then.

In long days gone by, I had thought of much simpler things, like what to wear to my brother's coronation: a gold dress or a blue one? Should I toss coins into Hecate's fountain for luck or take those coins and drop them over the cliff as an offering to the sea goddess? I longed for those simpler times, but as far as I knew, no creature had the power to go back in time. The past was forbidden to all. Yes, things had been simpler then.

My favorite treats then had been raisin cakes. And how I loved chasing my brother's chariots on my thin brown legs as he left for another victory. When I first met Cassander, I had loved him before I knew he had a beast's heart pounding in his chest.

I stood in silence beside Ramara and stared off, recalling with perfect clarity one particular day.

Greece, 1320 BC

"Alexander, Alexander! Please let me ride in the chariot with you. Look, I am dressed for it." I ran my hands over my white leather breastplate. It had been form-fitted for my birdlike body, and the leather worker had done an excellent job defining my muscles and figure. I had few curves, but the white leather made me appear strong and ready to do battle. Or so I thought.

"Out of the way now, Thessalonike." Roxana smiled down at me and took my hand, leading me from the golden carriage decked with blue ribbons. "You can wear your armor tonight at the banquet. Young Cassander will undoubtedly like seeing you look so fierce."

"You like it, Roxana?" I asked nervously. Her opinion mattered to me. Roxana was the most beautiful woman in the kingdom, and I wanted her approval. I wanted to be like her in every way.

Or I had. That was before. I remembered another day quite well.

It had been after Alexander had taken to his sick bed. He had returned to us from Babylon in a litter, arriving at night instead of in the middle of the day as had been planned. There were no victory parades, no train of elephants or other exotic animals. A mysterious fever struck him down and nearly took his life. But just as before, it could not kill him.

My brother seemed immortal. No matter how sick he was, he always recovered. I had no reason to think this would be any different. One day, I brought him fresh water and a small tray of food. He sat up and smiled when he saw me, and the sight of it filled my heart with joy.

"My own sister. How lovely you look today. Like a queen, but you are not yet a queen. What is taking Cassander so long?"

"He says he wants to build his kingdom before he takes me home to his land, brother. I respect him for that." I blushed as I put the tray in his lap.

"Time is precious, Nike." He bit into the green fruit and chewed, observing me carefully. "Did you know the Egyptian kings, pharaohs, do not marry commoners? They marry their sisters. What do you think of that?"

I laughed nervously. "Shocking!" I said as I poured his water. "How uncivilized, Alexander."

"Not so shocking, I think. It is good to be loved by your sister. See? Here you are, serving me water and fresh fruit. Here to care for me. Isn't that the best kind of love, sister?" I refused to look at him but instead walked away, leaving his question unanswered. Obviously the mysterious

Egyptian disease had him thinking crazy things. He would never have suggested such a thing to me before. I turned to call his servant when Roxana stood before me, blocking my way out of the bedchamber. Her dark hair hung loose around her shoulders, a golden headband crown upon her head. She had eyes that saw deep within my soul. I was afraid she had heard and misinterpreted Alexander's fevered words. I would never want to be the wife of my own brother. The idea disgusted me, as I knew it would Alexander if he were well.

"I, well, I brought him fruit and water. I'd better go now."

"Yes, I suppose you should, but maybe I should check your skirts first." Roxana stepped close to me and smelled the skin on my neck. "I can smell him on you, sister." I pulled away in surprise, my skin flushing bright red with embarrassment.

"Why do you say such things? Do you have a fever too?" I asked her, hoping she would finally move. I was backed against the table behind me, and there was nowhere else I could go. She would have to move so I could leave. Something here was wrong. Very wrong.

"You want it, don't you? He found it, did he tell you? The Immortal Waters! They are not just some old wives' tale. My brave husband found them, and now he's hiding them from me. We must not let him die, Thessalonike, must we? Would you be willing to help me heal him? We must force him to drink those waters. Where are they?"

"I do not know, sister-in-law. I swear to you." She didn't look like she believed me, but she said nothing. "But I will help you look for them. We must not let Alexander die."

"Very well, Thessalonike. I will hold you to your word. Come back tonight when the moon is full and high above the sea. I am depending on you."

"Yes, you can depend on me," I called behind me as I ran out of the room. What in the world was happening?

⁓ ❧ ⁓

"Hey!" Ramara called to me without looking back. He had removed the t-shirt he'd borrowed from me earlier, and his wings were half extended from his back.

So much for keeping a low profile, I thought. "What is it?"

"That ship. Do you hear that sound? Listen!"

"What are you—" I stopped immediately. I heard it too. I knew that song. That was the Mariner's Dirge, one of Roxana's songs. She did love her dirges. Although the boat was hundreds of yards away in the darkness, I could hear it plainly. I also heard the winds of a supernatural storm brewing out on the water, a storm created by an angry siren who was doing all she could to draw me into a fight. She was about to get her wish.

"You stay here, princess. Remember the Order's warning. Stay here."

"Sure," I lied to him. As soon as he dove into the water, I dove in behind him. Soon, Meri was beside me and we were racing together toward the boat with Ramara. My siren's hearing had returned. I could hear many familiar voices on the vessel. That was Captain Todd Stuckey's boat, the Hornet's Nest, and he was calling Mayday. Ramara burst out of the water, his wings unfurled fully now. I bobbed up quietly, aggravated that he would reveal our arrival so openly. I mean, I wanted Roxana to see me, know that I was coming, but I wanted to keep hidden from the humans on the boat. Ramara knew I was there, for he allowed me to hear his thoughts: "Damn spoiled princess."

"Hey, I can hear you, jerk."

"Then you should listen before you get these people hurt."

"I didn't start this, Ramara."

"No, but I am going to finish it right now, Thessalonike."

Roxana's dark head appeared above the waters. In a flat second she spotted me. She was glowing with power under the water near the bow of the boat. She tilted her head back and sang louder now; a vortex of wind and water responded and spun faster on the left side of the boat.

The boat creaked and popped as if it would burst into a thousand pieces in seconds. It listed so far at one point that I was certain it would sink.

"Stop this, Roxana! This is about you and me. Leave these humans alone."

She did not answer me but kept singing and winding her hands in a small circle, shaping the waves and the water. She slid slowly up out of the water; if I didn't know it was simply a trick, I would have thought she was standing on the waves. Her black gown clung to her lithe body, and her dark hair was plastered to her pale skin. I could feel her anger and hate.

"Enough of this," I said. With my mind, I summoned Meri who swam beneath me. "Call our friends, Meri." Immediately I felt waves of love hit me, and she began to seek targets in the water around us. A few seconds later those love waves then returned, and they slowed down Roxana's rage for a few seconds. That gave me enough time to come up with another idea.

"Meri!" She popped up beside me looking fierce, her eyes vivid and deep blue now. She stared at Roxana, who continued to manipulate the water and wind with her fingers. "Send your love toward the men in the boat. I will help you! Let's do it on the count of three! 1- 2- 3!" I did not have the precise ability that Meri did, but I focused on our task and offered a wave of love to them.

Heavy waves of love struck the men, and I could feel their fear dissipate despite their dangerous circumstances. As they fell under our spell, I began to sing a love song against Roxana without worrying that I would enchant them. My song would weaken her power temporarily and eventually stop her magic's influence if I could just maintain my focus. Meri's love waves would protect the men and keep them spellbound long enough for me to counteract my enemy siren's song. We sang against one another for a few minutes, and Meri never let up on her love waves.

I did not know how we would break this standoff, but I could not back down now. Slowly we began to drift toward one another. Suddenly, Ramara dove from the sky and hit the deck with a crash. I screamed in surprise and heard Roxana laugh as she disappeared under the waves.

The storm stopped raging, the waters grew calm and I climbed like a madwoman onto the boat. "No, Meri. It is too dangerous. Stay in the water." Some of the crew lay on the deck of the boat as if they were still experiencing Meri's seductive love. I found Ramara lying on the deck; his wings were retracted now, thankfully, but he was knocked out cold. I slapped him in his face hoping he would wake. After a few seconds, he did.

"So you do care..." he flirted with me.

"What?" Then it dawned on me. He wouldn't have been protected by Meri's love waves. He heard my song loud and clear, and he'd been enchanted. No wonder he fell out of the sky like a rock.

"I knew you wanted me," he purred, pawing at my wet breasts.

Slapping his hands away, I said, "You knocked yourself stupid. What kind of move was that, eloi? You could have killed yourself, not to mention drowned the crew. Don't you know how to protect yourself from a siren's song?"

"It worked, didn't it? Help me up," he said in a sexy voice.

Embarrassed, I stood up and shook my head. "Help yourself and get yourself together. We have to get out of here."

The captain walked over to us on drunken legs with a goofy grin on his face. It was clear he was still under the influence of the mermaid's enchantment. Hm...that might work in our favor.

"What happened?" he asked, slurring his words. "I mean, I saw what happened, but I can't believe it. Was he flying? Is he dead?"

"Um, no. He's alive. He didn't fall far. We were in the chopper above you. Didn't you see us?"

"What chopper? I didn't see any chopper."

"Well, I was in it with my friend Ramar—I mean, Ray here. We thought we could rescue you, but the storm was too much for me. Ray fell out, and I crashed the chopper. But I'm a new pilot, so... I probably shouldn't have tried landing on your boat during a storm." I spoke in a soft, monotone voice, hoping to extend the magic a bit. Ramara stared at me in complete disbelief.

The captain blinked at me, his mind struggling with what he had seen. He said, "Well, you were close. Thank you for trying, Nik. It was a brave thing to do. Talk about a squall. Hey, you okay, buddy? Ray, is it? Lost your shirt and shoes, huh? Well, it could have been worse. Hey, Gates! Do a head count! Is everyone okay?"

He walked off like he'd been hit with fairy dust, if you believed in that sort of thing. It had been a long time since I had planted memories, but it seemed to work.

Ramara stood close to me and whispered. I could hear him plainly now that the wind had died and the water had calmed. "I can't believe he bought that ridiculous story."

"I can't believe you didn't have enough sense to protect yourself from a siren's song. I mean, how are you going to protect me if you can't even manage that?"

"A funny siren. That's a new one." He shook his head and arched his back against some obvious pain he wasn't up to admitting. "How about letting me make up the ridiculous stories from now on. Who's going to believe that you're a pilot?"

"Do you know what year it is, eloi? Women do things like fly now."

"I do know what year it is, but that doesn't mean a thing. Some things never change. I have never met a woman who could properly drive a chariot or anything else."

"That's it. I'm going home, jerk. See you later. Why don't you make up a story about where I went? Or is that too easy for you?"

Before waiting for an answer, I dove into the water. Meri put her arm around me, and together we swam back to my home. Once we arrived I felt less angry but tired. Very tired. I surfaced and sat on the sand, allowing my gills to empty.

"You did good, Meri. What would I do without my friend? You are my family. Keep to yourself and stay close. This has just begun, I am afraid."

She sent me a wave of love, then with a sweet smile dove into the water and disappeared. The sun would come up soon, and I would have to go to work to maintain my human appearance. I thought of Cruise again. Everything had changed. I had to have time. Time to think about Jack. Time to grieve for him and then weigh whether or not I wanted to pursue a relationship with another human. Wasn't it all useless? And so unfair?

I went inside and peeked in on the drunken goddess, who had changed positions but was still sound asleep. I showered and got into my pajamas before climbing into Jack's bed, the bed we used to share before we began to pretend I was his granddaughter.

Tears filled my eyes as I remembered a few things, like how hard I tried to hide the truth from him. But he was smart and knew all about siren mythology. He had been a notable scholar in his time. I also remembered how he had wanted to travel and I encouraged him to do so, but I could not go with him. I could never leave Dauphin Island or Sirens Gate. I was its protector. Nobody could use the gate without express permission from the Order. Too much was at stake. He had left, but he never stayed away for too long. Except for once. He'd come back older, tired and sick. The disease had taken him, and there was nothing I could do about it.

The heartache was too great. Too hard to bear. I could not watch him die. I had failed him in that. I sent the request to slumber to the Order, and they had given permission. Heliope had appeared and placed her hand on me, casting the sleep spell. It wasn't really sleep. Only your memory slept. I continued to live with Jack but as his granddaughter. He'd cut my hair short and introduced me to everyone as his long-lost relative. Nobody was the wiser. He lived a few more years, but they were bittersweet.

Jack, I am sorry. I failed you. I could not save you. I drew up the quilt around my neck and sobbed quietly. I could almost smell his cedar cologne and his pipe tobacco, hear the steady drum of his heart beating.

Finally I cried myself to sleep and dreamed of Jack.

Chapter Ten—Meri

D*own Deep*
Friend had awakened, and all was well again. I forgot all about my previous loneliness. It was like it never happened because we were sisters of the heart. I had not yet told her my idea, that we should go home. It seemed less likely that she would now, but I would not give up yet. I would find a way to ask her, to convince her.

This was not a safe place for her. Or for me. Maybe Mother Minerva would help us. If I asked correctly. Although my mother, the Great Minerva, had many daughters, I considered none of them my sisters. They had abandoned me, fearing Minerva's wrath more than they loved me.

I tried to explain to them my gnawing need to serve the new siren, but they did not care. If only I had not followed her so fervently while she was still a human. As if it were my fault that she had been changed. The change had saved her. Dionysus had saved her from death and had given me a friend. I would never speak ill of him for that. Although I did not serve him directly, I held no ill feelings toward him. Not as Minerva and the other mermaids did.

And that made me an outsider. An outcast. Of all the dozens of golden-haired mermaids that swam the seas, only I had abandoned my home to serve—no, befriend—a siren. I was a shame to my kind. Mermaids had an ability that most Oceanids did not. We befriended for life. We protected. We watched over our friends. I had only one. My Friend.

Yes, I had seen her before her great fall from the cliff of Meteora. She often swam in the azure waters off the coast near her father's palace. She was never alone but always seemed to be alone. I understood that. To some she appeared as just one of the many Greek royal beauties who enjoyed life at court, but I saw something in her.

All of Macedonia and Greece whispered her name. In fact, it was on everyone's lips, at least the ones I heard around the harbor. A great beauty ready to marry. I had to see her, and when I found her, I watched her constantly. What must it have been like to be so loved, to be so beautiful? No one had ever called me beautiful. I occasionally looked at myself in the calm pools of water near the harbor, and I was not a hag, but I was not beautiful.

I remembered one day in particular. Hidden in one of my secret spots in the rocks, I shooed birds away and listened to the girls whisper about the latest conquest of Alexander and Cassander. I heard stories of Ptolemy at the Battle of Ezira. How he'd stormed the front line of the enemy in such a frenzy he'd forgotten to put on his clothes. I noticed that even though many of the girls her age seemed preoccupied with court intrigues, such as who stole a casket of the new queen's emeralds, Friend did not offer much to their conversation. She cared not that Ptolemy had the largest sword or that Cassander had lovely brown eyes. She smiled her careful smile and sank beneath the waters like she wanted to wash them all away. I understood her disappointment in the world she found herself in. I felt the same way.

She saw me once. I hovered too near, too close to the group of giggling girls as they swam in their knee-length sheer gowns with their cascades of long hair trailing behind them like seaweed. I had not expected the sister of Alexander to dive that deeply. Most of the girls did not swim like she did. They were happy to stay on the surface, splashing one another and complaining when someone else did the same.

After our encounter, she'd burst to the surface gasping for air while I swam with all my might back to the white stone rocks nearby. Panting for breath myself, I clung to the warm stones for a few minutes before I disappeared into the deep water. Friend told the other girls what she saw, but they hadn't believed her.

A mermaid!

Of course nobody believed her. No mermaid had been seen for over a hundred years. Fanciful girl, they called her. Good for me. I never wanted to become the pet of some spoiled princess, which I probably would have been if I had showed myself openly. I would never forget the moment we saw one another. It must have been a shock for her to see me, a small, unimpressive mermaid who had invaded her swimming pool.

After that, I could do nothing but follow her from afar, but she searched for me. I would see her scanning the waters and would duck away. I do not know why I was so curious about her. So drawn to her. It would be interesting to meet a land-girl, I thought. I tried to reason with Minerva, to explain what I felt and why, but she would not listen. She cared nothing for my feelings and did not understand my interest in Friend but scolded me for being spotted. If it happened again I would be punished. I might even be caged and kept from swimming in the open water.

That had been so long ago. My thoughts continued along this line as I swam into the waters where all the above light vanished and the chill seeped into your bones. It was so empty here between the world above and the world below. Yet just a few more feet and I would be as close to my home as I ever would be. The heavy metal would be closed to me. It would stay closed forever. Minerva did not forgive such serious offenses as mine. I had made my choice. She showed no mercy.

Over time I had returned here many times, sending waves of love into the darkness, but no pale face ever came to greet me. No mermaid-kind would acknowledge me or allow me entry. A few more pumps of water, and I made it to my home, the black gates still locked in place, a faint light in the distance. This was only one entrance, but it served as a reminder that I was still not welcome. I peered at the light. It was proof that life did continue without this particular daughter of Minerva.

Sadly I thought of Sasha, Myray and Meera, the mermaids who were once my companions. I moaned and grasped the gate with both hands and rubbed my forehead against the unforgiving steel.

"Minerva," I called to my mother with my mind. Once upon a time, she would hear me as soon as I spoke her name. I did not feel that connection now, but I had to try. "Danger has come again, Mother. Roxana has the bones, and this is the last gate. She will make him live again and destroy the gate. Blood is required, my Friend's blood. Help Friend, please."

No answer came. I shook the gate, but it did not budge. She could help. She *should* help. Friend needed her help. I called again, "Minerva," but there came no answer. Only the slithering of a large eel, a Protector who eyed me threateningly as my hands futilely worked at the lock. He hung near now, ever closer, and I sent my most persuasive wave of love to him. There was no acknowledgment and no change in his movements. If anything, he appeared more aggressive now. I backed away from the gate, feeling hopeless.

Our last battle with Roxana had been tough, nearly impossible. How much stronger would she be now that so much time had passed and her frustration grew? We needed help. More than just Ramara. Then it occurred to me.

We had an ally. A forgotten ally. Heliope would not be pleased, but this was for Friend's good. She would see that eventually. Yes, this was a good ally and a very good idea.

Now all I had to do was retrieve him.

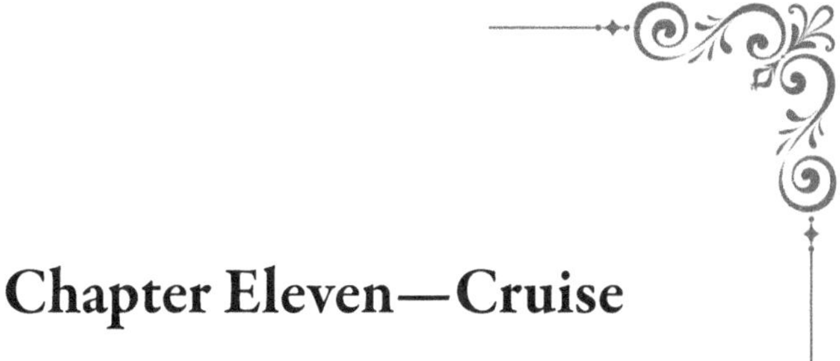

Chapter Eleven—Cruise

Crooked Heart

The fist slapping the screen door repeatedly reverberated through my head like a guitarist who knew only one note. I stumbled away from the coffeepot, the heavy set of squad room keys jangling noisily at my side. I felt like I had when I was sixteen, the day after I took a high school dare and drank a whole bottle of crappy strawberry wine. Yep, that's how wonderful I felt right this moment. I set the cup of piping hot coffee down on the counter and shuffled to the back door, rubbing my red eyes with my knuckle.

I recognized Lucy's black hair and pale skin right away, even without getting a good look at her face through the dingy lace curtain. "What's up?" I was surprised to find her on my doorstep.

"Somebody broke into the Pirateer last night. Took a truckload of booze. I'm ruined if we can't find it!"

Rubbing my hands over my face, I tried to make sense of what she was telling me. What the hell was wrong with me? "Did you call the station? Make a report?"

"Why would I do that? I'm here! Now get your ass moving and come see. This really sucks, Cruise. Do you know how much this is going to cost the bar? Geesh, I hate spring break."

The old landline phone rang on the wall. Oh God, the noise. I raised a finger to Lucy and answered it. "Castille."

"Hey, we've got a murder. You think you can be bothered to show up and help us out?"

"Murder? Who's dead?"

"I've been trying to call you for an hour. Roll your ass out of bed and get down to Chaumont, on the bay side. Down by the old pool."

"Chaumont? Is Nik okay?"

"As far as I know. Now get here!"

"On the way." I hung up the phone with a shaking hand. What a jerk! How in the hell could he have been calling me for an hour? I'd been awake. Kind of. I grabbed my cell phone and groaned when I saw it was dead. In my drunken stupor, I'd forgotten to charge it last night. Speaking of drunken…. "What the hell was in that drink? What was it called, Witches Brew? I only took a sip and I'm still feeling it."

"You are such a wimp. Are you coming or not? I can't get the chief to the bar, and I want to file a report."

"Sorry, Lucy, but you'll have to wait. There's been a murder. I have to head over to Chaumont."

"Murder? Who? Are you kidding me? I can't remember the last time someone died on this island." She chewed the inside of her lip and stared at me.

"Don't know who yet. Come on, I have to go. You know I can't tell you anything about an open investigation."

She touched her finger to my face and pulled the skin under my eye down to stare into it. "You know, you really do need to leave the booze alone. You don't look so hot."

"Thanks for the advice. Listen, don't disturb the crime scene at the bar. I'll be there as soon as I'm done with this. Take pictures and secure the bar, but don't do anything else. Got it?"

She nodded. "Aye, aye, captain." Then she quickly stood on her tiptoes and kissed me on the mouth. She whispered, "I'm glad it's not you." Without another word she left me standing in the kitchen, slapping the door one last time before she left. She sped away on her moped, and I watched her from the doorway, my head throbbing and my hands sweating. That kiss wasn't supposed to happen, but I'd have to deal with this situation later.

My first murder, and I didn't hear the radio call. Yes, this I couldn't think about right now. I'd have to let her down easy. Lucy could be a wildcat when something didn't go her way. And I wasn't going her way at all. I liked her as a friend but nothing else. Dang, I didn't need this kind of complication in my life right now.

I turned off the coffeepot, grabbed my coffee and walked to the car. Sliding the key into the ignition, I wondered what she was talking about. Glad what wasn't me? I shook my head and blinked, trying to clear the fog. I turned off Cadillac Drive onto Chaumont and eased down the street. I eyeballed Nik's house. The windows were closed now and her bike was gone.

Must have gone to work. At the end of the street, two cars from the Mobile County Sheriff's Department, Belloc's SUV and the coroner's sedan waited on me. Nosy Mrs. Bannister stood on her porch in her scruffy pink robe watching it all. I put the car in park, slapped my hat on my head and walked toward the crime scene.

"Officer Castille, you remember Darwin Lamplighter, our new coroner? And you know these guys."

I couldn't remember their names, but I nodded as one of them gave me a halfhearted "What's up?" They didn't care for coming across the bridge too much. I knew for a fact Dan Belloc didn't like including them. The Mobile County Sheriff's Department had more deputies than a pack of dogs had fleas.

"Morning, deputies. Dr. Lamplighter." I squatted down beside Chief Belloc and watched as he pulled back the tarp that covered the body lying in the road. What I saw almost knocked the breath out of me. That was Lloyd Joshua, the island's postmaster and only mailman. He was wearing the same clothing he'd worn last night: khaki pants, a light blue oxford and a dark blue windbreaker that had his initials on the collar. His topsider shoes were missing, and so was his watch. He'd been proud of that watch, a thank-you gift from the town after twenty years of service. I made myself look at his face.

"When was he found?"

"About an hour ago. Mrs. Bannister says she went out to get her paper and found Lloyd like this. Don't see his mail truck around, and there's no sign of his shoes." Lloyd's tanned face was pale but not white. His skin had a strange blue tint to it; even his lips were blue. Like he hadn't gotten any air at all.

"So the theory is he walked down here barefoot and died in the driveway?" one of the officers joked as he smacked on a piece of gum.

"You fellas need something official right now?" I asked them as I stood up.

"Can't leave without it. In case you haven't heard, we've got a new chief of police, and he's got a hard-on for murder cases. Wants the coroner's prelim COD ASAP."

With bleary eyes I stared at them and said, "I'm sure there are other murders to investigate, if this even is a murder. I still don't get why you're here. We could send you the documents."

"Just had to see for ourselves is all. Breaking in the new kid. So what's the word, Lamplighter? The postmaster went for a barefooted stroll and decided to die right here?"

Darwin Lamplighter stroked his awful mustache and studied the body for another minute. He pulled the tarp back over Lloyd's face and gave us a hesitant look. "Unofficially?"

"Yep, unofficially is fine, doc. Nobody here is going to hold your feet to the fire on this one," Belloc said, standing up beside me. "And this isn't usually how we do things, Lou. Let's not make this a habit."

Dr. Lamplighter cleared his throat and pulled a small tube of antibacterial liquid from his pocket. "I think this man was poisoned. His nail beds are discolored, and that shade of blue isn't from manual strangulation—not to mention there are no marks on his neck. From my preliminary examination I have found no cuts, bruises or bullet holes. He's the right age for a heart attack, but those fingernails are dead giveaways. Pardon the pun."

"Pun?" Belloc asked stupidly.

"Yes, you see I was…never mind. I'll get Mr. Joshua to my office now, if you don't mind."

"Not at all. Do what you need to, doc. Castille, come with me. You two give the doc a hand, will you?"

They didn't want to, but they didn't argue with Chief Belloc. That was smart because he could be a real ass if you picked a fight with him. "You know anything about this?" he asked me.

"I don't know how he got here. He was at the Pirateer last night, daydreaming about the bartender. I left before he did. I went home and passed out."

"Passed out? Where you driving drunk? You sure you didn't get hammered with Lloyd?"

"Hell no. I don't drink. Much. You know that. When I left, he was sipping on a drink and hoping to talk with Lucy."

Belloc flicked a toothpick into the sandy roadway. "All roads lead to you then, don't they? Mrs. Bannister says you were down here spying on her with binoculars last night. Any truth to that?"

I couldn't think of a thing to say that didn't sound ridiculous. I waved my hand dismissively.

He laughed nervously. "Yeah, I suppose you're right. Who'd want to spy on her? But what were you doing out here? Did you see anything?"

I toyed with the idea of telling the chief about the shadow that flew over my car but decided against it. He already thought I was a slacker for missing his call earlier. If I told him about a giant batlike shadow, he might have had me drug tested. No, I'd tell him the truth. Or at least part of it.

"Nike Augustine and I had a date last night." I stepped closer to him so the others couldn't hear us. They were lifting Lloyd's body and moving him to the gurney now. I turned my head and focused on Dan. "When I went to pick her up, she wasn't there. Some lady claiming to be her Aunt Helen came to the door and said Nik wouldn't make it. Some kind of family crisis. I tried calling her, but she didn't answer. I guess I got carried away. I rode down here and thought I'd sit on the house a while, just to make sure everything was okay. I didn't see Lloyd until I went to the bar after that."

"Helen? I didn't know she had an Aunt Helen."

"Me either. That's why I was worried."

"Hey, I'm not saying you did the right thing. Spying on the girl isn't the way to handle things. Sometimes a man has to take no for an answer, Cruise. No means no."

"No means—look, I didn't try to force anyone to do anything. I've just never heard of this lady, is all. So I watched the place for a while. Then I left. Lucy at the Pirateer can vouch for me."

"Fine, you weren't being a pervert. Go see if she's home now. If she's not, check up at the souvenir shop. I'd like to know if that's related and if maybe this Aunt Helen might know something. I'll finish Mrs. Bannister's report on Joshua first. Meet you at the station when I'm done."

"Got it, chief." I left without saying anything to the county deputies, but I made sure I waved at Mrs. Bannister before I left. Nosy old bat. The old, less mature Cruise would have dumped a truckload of feral cats on her doorstep as a thank you. Pulling the car in front of the faded white picket fence, I hesitated for a moment and then put the new squad car in park. I walked through the rock garden to Nik's front door. Nothing looked out of place. The door used to be light blue, but like the fence, it needed a good paint job.

Paint didn't last long here on the island. I knocked once, then twice, but nobody answered. I walked around back, but the back door was locked. The kitchen window was open but the screen was secure, and I didn't see anyone moving around in there. I could smell fresh coffee. That was a good sign, I told myself as I fought the panic rising in my chest. She had to be all right. What kind of criminal stuck around to make coffee after he committed his crimes? I got back in the car and rode the quarter mile to Shipwreck Souvenirs.

Nik's pink and white bicycle was parked on the side of the building, and I could see that something had been in her garbage again. The animal had made such a mess that it was clearly visible from the road. I wasn't offering to pick up the trash again. Not today.

I pulled in the front parking lot and left the lights on for effect. At least she'd know I was on official business and not acting like a nosy pervert.

Not like last night, right? Geesh. Here I am worried sick, and she's perfectly fine. Looking beautiful. Damn, I'm a loser.

"Good morning," I greeted her, trying to sound as official as possible.

"Good morning, Cruise." She stopped in the middle of pushing the cash drawer in, and the register bell dinged. It sounded ridiculously loud. "I haven't made coffee yet."

"Didn't come for coffee. Are you okay?" Then in a worried rush of words I said, "I met your Aunt Helen. She says that there was some kind of family crisis. You know I would have been there for you, if you'd just tell me." To my surprise she didn't try to argue with me or defend herself. Instead she turned her back to me and began filling baskets with seashell coin purses. "Hey, did you hear me? There's a dead guy on your street, so excuse me if I'm a little concerned about you."

She dropped the purses and faced me. I could tell she'd been crying. *What was going on?* Her eyes were more blue than gray, and that always happened whenever she got teary-eyed. I never saw anyone else like that. It was one of the things that made her so unique. That and her perfume, which drove me nuts. "Someone died on Chaumont?"

"The postmaster, Lloyd Joshua. Mrs. Bannister found his body this morning in her driveway."

"Oh my God. That's horrible." She shoved the basket into the cubicle behind her counter and turned to face me again. She looked too calm, too still. "He seemed like a nice man."

"What is going on, Nik? Or should I call you Thessalonike? Who is Aunt Helen?" The hair on my arms stood up, and my mouth felt drier than it had when I woke up this morning. "Say something." I was pretty worried now. Even if she didn't want to date me, we'd been friends since I moved here. Was she going to throw that away?

"Stop, Cruise! You can't help me with this. Listen, I have a big family. But it's really complicated, and I don't even know how to begin to explain it."

"Explain what, Nik?" I reached for her hand, and she didn't pull away. "What is it? You're a gypsy? You're a criminal? What is it?" My typical humor wasn't working.

She slid her hand away, patting me once, and said in a flat tone, "It's going to be okay and you have to trust me." She stared me in the eyes, and I felt my skin crawl again.

"What is this? Some kind of Jedi mind trick?" Before she could respond, the old-fashioned front door bell rang and in walked a man I knew I hadn't seen before. He had to be six four, totally built, and his face was striking. He had shoulder-length brown hair, but he didn't look like a sissy. Not one bit. He was strong, and not just gym strong either. He glanced at me but kept his focus on Nik.

"We have to go," he said to her. She looked from me to him and reached for her purse under the counter.

"Go where?" I asked, exasperated.

Slinging the purse on her shoulder she spoke again in that unusually calm voice. "You have to trust me, Cruise. I will be okay."

"Stop talking like a damn robot and tell me what's going on. I'm the cop here."

The man laughed at her. "That's not going to work. We have to go."

"Goodbye, Cruise." She practically shoved me out the door, and I stood stupidly watching her lock it. I couldn't shake the feeling that this would be the last time I saw her. "I can't see you anymore. I want you to forget me. I mean it." She left her bike and went walking down the road with the stranger. I watched them clear Targetti's and Spinner's Seafood. Standing with my hands on my hips, I tried to shake off the residue of last night and the heartbreak of today.

My crazy father had been right all along. Women were different than men. They had crooked hearts.

Chapter
Twelve—Ramara

B*attle Lines*
What in the world did she see in the human? Or half-human. He wasn't too bright if he didn't even realize that he had supernatural DNA inside him. Definitely wasn't too tall. "I'm not impressed," I confessed in a low voice.

Without missing a beat she said, "Do you need to be impressed?"

"He's not worthy of you."

She made a sound that let me know she didn't want to talk about it. "What is so important that you had to out me in front of him?"

"Out you? I do not understand the phrase. Forgive me. I have been elsewhere for the past fifty years. You know, while you were playing house with that other human. Sirens are fickle creatures."

"Don't be bitter because you haven't experienced love, Ramara."

"I take offense at that."

"You'll take offense at anything you don't understand, and quite frankly I don't care right now." We walked toward the water's edge and then walked toward the gloomy-looking motel. Such a far cry from my last assignment in Versailles. The walk took us out of the way a bit, but being near the water was good for both of us. Probably a good idea to change the subject. Perhaps I wasn't as well versed in love as the princess was, but I did know what love felt like. I had loved before. Should I point that out? Probably not. She didn't seem like she was in the mood to talk about personal matters.

"You will never believe who washed up on shore this morning. I don't know how he found his way here—that's not true. It had to be your pet. Only a mermaid could have released him. It's Agrios. Heliope is going to blow a ringer."

"You mean a gasket, and Meri is not my pet. She's my friend." She smiled despite her irritation and focused her mesmerizing eyes on me. "Are you serious now? It truly is Agrios?"

"I am always serious, princess."

"I have asked you before to call me by my name, Nike or Thessalonike. Not princess. It is the modern age, Ramara."

"What about Nik? May I call you that?"

"Um no. Only my friends call me that."

"I see."

"Don't act hurt. I am no one important, and just because we see one another a few times a century doesn't make us actual friends."

"That is also painful to hear. I have few friends."

She slung her drooping purse over her shoulder and peered at me cautiously through her long bangs. "If you mean that, I am sorry. I guess I wasn't ready to remember yet, but here we are again. At least it's you and not some god-awful Muse."

"I hear there aren't too many of those anymore. Like the Tritoni. They have almost disappeared."

"I wouldn't worry too much. Knowing muses, they're probably gathered together trying to outsing one another. They make children seem like intellects."

I had to laugh in agreement. "Well, you must be important to the grand scheme of things or the Order would not have sent me to protect you."

"There are no Macedonian kingdoms here—I have no illusions that I am all that important. The only thing important about me, at least in the eyes of the Order, is the blood that flows through my veins. Funny, isn't it? All that science that the world now knows about, everything people know about DNA, and the battle for my DNA continues. And, in point of fact, the Order did not send you here to protect me. That's not your primary task, is it? It's the Sirens Gate. It is the last one. If Roxana destroys it, there will be no chance for anyone to use it again. That's it. Finito, as the Italians say."

That reminded me of my encounter with Faydra, and of the ominous letter that showed up in Nike's home. The tension in the air increased, and I could not shake the feeling that we were being watched. Not from the skies, for I would have seen anyone approach. The sky was cloudless and the air was still except for the southerly breeze. I missed the smell of orange trees and the sprinkling of fountains. I missed home, suddenly. Perhaps Faydra had been right. I was too old for this. Maybe I should have given up my wings when I had the chance.

Shaking her head, Thessalonike asked, "Where did you stash Agrios? Why would Meri bring him here, if that's truly what happened?"

"I don't know why she would. Perhaps the mermaid meant to give him as a gift. He's in my room, but I don't know how long I can keep him quiet. He was sleeping when I left, thankfully. Since he wasn't quite himself yet, I was able to use a minor enchantment to control him, but he will be stronger from his long confinement. And who can tell what kind of mood he will be in? These so-called gods have bad attitudes; even though nobody much remembers them anymore, they act as if the whole world owes them something.

That goes double for Agrios. Such a proud little man. You know how one of them is when he comes out of confinement. All he thinks about is drinking, eating and...um, women. I'm not here to guard him. I'm here to protect you—and then the gate," I corrected her. Why was I telling her this? Would I really put her before the gate? Odd that I would want to. "This way," I said gruffly as we walked up the rickety stairs.

I led her past a row of doors at the Summer Breeze Motel. "So what's the plan here?" she asked. "I can't go up there. You say he has been confined with no female companionship? No way am I going in that room. He'll be on me before I can say my name. I'll stay outside while you make sure he hasn't torn the place down. Then we'll come up with some kind of plan."

"If he is willing to help us, Agrios has the power to turn tides. That could come in handy. From my initial contact with Roxana, I can see that she plans to play on the water. I wasn't sure she would."

"I never doubted it. That and the Drago constellation is above us tonight. I think we'll have to stop her sooner rather than later. I wonder why after all this time she wants to try again? Wasn't Alexander's last resurrection disastrous enough? And why would the Order leave such an important matter to us and not back us up?"

"Because they can't. I think—oh no! Just a minute." I heard something crash in my room. Obviously my charge was awake now. Awake and throwing a tantrum. Sliding the key in the door, I raised my arm to protect myself from any blow that might come my way. Agrios acted first and thought about it afterwards. "Hey! Agrios, it's me! Ramara." One crash later, I was inside and had him by his arm. From the look of the room he'd had quite a temper tantrum. I heard Thessalonike speaking to someone outside. I held Agrios by the throat now to keep him from shouting at me. "Shh. Will you keep quiet?"

The motel manager, someone she obviously knew, was yelling at her, but it didn't last long. Her mesmerizing voice calmed the situation, and soon he was trotting down the stairs back to wherever he came from. Agrios sniffed the air. "A siren...how long it's been. Please, send her in."

"I will not. That is Thessalonike, not one of your playthings, Agrios. Now calm yourself down if you can." He had not changed much. Still short with a head of brown curls. I'd heard some women over the years call him handsome, but I didn't see it. He had overly large lips and slightly bulbous brown eyes. Probably swollen from all the wine he drank. He was the patron of wine, after all. He took his job seriously, but his philandering ways often got in the way. Including with goddesses like Heliope. He'd wined her for years before she consented to be his consort. He stole her from Philip and, once he claimed her, cast her off like a broken old sandal.

Agrios had no love for Philip or his children, but he'd been mandated to protect them. They were not the children of Heliope—or Olympia, as she had been known prior to her exalted position as goddess—but he hated them no less. Yet, despite himself, he loved Heliope, or so he told everyone who would listen back then. Who knew how he felt now? Gods never loved like lower beings. *Thinking about love again, are we? Perhaps I should cast off my wings and grab a lyre.*

"What do you mean by dragging me here? I have nothing to do with any of this. If I can't roam free, then at least let me go back to my confinement."

"I think you've sulked enough. We have a crisis. Now. This moment. I can't endure any more of your theatrics, puny man. Now can we move this along?" I released his arm and looked at him sternly. "The mermaid Meri brought you here to help Thessalonike, although I personally don't see much value in you—or any cast-off god," I growled at him as I stood a few inches from his face. "But you have a part to play in this, Agrios. Roxana wants to activate the gate for Alexander. I have orders to protect the princess and keep the gate sealed. It is not his time, if it ever will be." Unafraid, he stepped past me, walked toward the window and stood staring at the girl. He licked his lips as he watched her. She wasn't looking at us but kept her focus on the crashing waves. Her slim body leaned against the railing. A squall was brewing over the west end of the island, and she watched it with her steely gray eyes.

"I thirst. I need wine and lots of it. If they have that here. Where am I? I do not recognize this shoreline." His voice was quiet and thoughtful. Never good.

"You are in the southern part of the United States, on a barrier island. Dauphin Island, it is called now; it was once Massacre Island. Do you remember where they kept you? What crime did you commit last?"

"Why? Is that any of your concern, eloi? Can you bring me wine, or do I need to speak to the siren? Perhaps I will go myself and find some. It has been a long time since I explored anywhere new."

"I will get you what you want, but you cannot tear the place down, Agrios. This is a very small island, and we have strict orders to remain anonymous."

A sneaky smile spread across his face, but he did not turn his gaze away from Thessalonike. I grew angrier by the moment as I watched him leering at her. "Anonymous. Your orders, eloi. Not mine."

I grunted in indignation. "Fair enough. But what will Heliope say when I tell her you assaulted her charge?"

"Heliope is here in this godforsaken place?" His eyes widened with a mixture of delight and wariness.

"Yes, and I'm sure she will be happy to see you."

That broke his attention from the princess. I stood tall and erect, hoping he would challenge me openly so I could throttle him. "I advise you to bring me that wine soon. The drunker I'll be, the better. For everyone."

"Stay here. Don't venture out. It's not safe. There are many kinds of creatures here, and none of them will be happy to see you. You are, after all, no longer in charge."

"Is anyone?" he asked. It was the first serious question of the night.

"I guess we will see."

He smiled stupidly. "And sooner than you think. I suggest you put the enchantment back on the door. I feel reasonable at the moment, but you and I both know that won't last. I'm not the god of wine and drunken women for nothing."

"I'll be back soon. I'll get your wine, but I want your word that you will help her if she needs it."

"Oh, I give you my word. Bring me wine now."

I didn't feel any better. What was a god's promise worth? Not much.

I walked outside, bowed my head and spoke the enchantment over the lock. Thessalonike saw him but did not acknowledge him. "You were right. Stay away from him as long as you can. He hasn't changed much. Let's walk and talk. I have to get him wine. Where can I go to find this?"

"Um, package store. It's back that way, past my shop. Right at the bridge. I'm going to see Meri and then Heliope. She's going to love this bit of news. What was Meri thinking? Why him?"

"Probably because he was the closest. There is a veiled island south of here. I'm sure that's where he was sent. Some dalliance with a high-ranking rage, although he wouldn't admit it. After all this time, he's still a piece of work."

"Why would he help me, Ramara? I don't understand. He never liked me, not in a real way. Only as a potential sexual partner, and that was never going to happen."

"Because he can't allow that gate to be destroyed any more than any of the rest of the Order can. I don't pretend to understand it all, but those gates are tied somehow to their power. It's always been a balancing act between the races. Those gates were kind of the tiebreakers. Now there's just the one here for our kind. The air folk have two, and I can't tell you more than that."

She shook her head a little. "It's funny how I was sent here to protect it but I don't know a thing about it. I guess they want it that way. I am tired of being a pawn in a game that I don't understand. It's been that way forever, even when my brother lived—the first time. Did anyone ever care about me?"

I don't know why, but I put my arms around her. She didn't fight me. I hugged her briefly and stepped back. I had to find the wine. "I'll tend to this one. I don't dare walk him around the island, though. Can you bring Heliope here? The gate isn't far. I don't know when they will come, but they are coming. Let's be there when they show up."

"Sounds like a plan. I'll be back before sundown."

She walked away, but I didn't watch her, as much as I might have liked to. I had to intoxicate Agrios. And quickly.

I cheated on this trip across the island. I walked blindingly fast, so fast that no one except another supernaturate would detect me. To me they appeared as stock-still images while the human world looked like an oil painting that had melted in high temperatures. I counted six so far. Two harpies, a sleeping vampire—she was buried deep under the jail—and three others that I could not quite detect. They had human helpers. Those I could detect easily enough. They carried traces of the supes on them, traces transferred only through communion, regular communion. Witches! There were witches on this island. I spat on the ground before walking into the store.

The shirt Thessalonike gave me from her store was too snug. It had a ridiculous open-mouthed shark on the front with the words, "You're going to need a bigger boat." Whatever that meant.

I walked into Fred's Discount Liquors and didn't see a soul.

A dusty television monitor displayed my image on the screen. I supposed this was meant to discourage theft, but all it did for me was make me stand taller until I walked past the screen. That was a weakness of mine, looking at myself. Not because I was in love with my own looks. I wasn't Narcissus. The obsession was more like I wanted to make sure I hadn't changed yet. I'd come close to slipping to the other side after I took a human wife. Every time I saw myself these days, I thanked my lucky stars that it was not a demon's face I saw. If that happened to me, I would fly as high as I could and then simply fall to the ground. Great falls didn't always kill eloi, but it would be worth a try.

I opened the cooler door and saw nothing but beer. Imported, domestic, flavored and even blue. Who ever heard of blue beer? These humans and their wacky ways. No red wine there. As I searched for wine and intentionally avoided the monitors, I totally forgot that I was alone. I had money. The Order had provided me with everything I needed. Then my hackles began to creep and I knew that somewhere close to me, very close indeed, was another supernatural creature. And she was one I was familiar with. I heard her voice before I saw her.

"Ra-ma-ra," her whisper reached my ears, and it immediately filled me with both rage and desire. Unfortunate for her. Arousal made me strong—twice as strong as I normally would be.

"It cannot be." I swung my head around, two bottles of wine in my hand. She stood in the doorway to what I assumed was the stock room with a delicious smile on her face.

"It can be. And it can be just like old times, Ra-ma-ra." She wore her hair short, in the modern style. Her expressive eyes and sultry voice almost mesmerized me, but she was no siren or rage. This was Nemesis. My Nemesis.

The Order had lied. She wasn't bound on any veiled island. She was right here! She'd been here the whole time.

"No, never. It will never be like old times for us, Nemesis."

My answer did not please her, for she took off running toward me. She screamed as she descended on me, her wings expanded, knocking over bottles of liquor, wine and beer. I felt another presence—this was a witch. Her witch. She'd stepped into the shop from the store room whispering incantations. I laughed as they fell off me like paper chains, but she did not quit. As Nemesis and I struggled with one another, throwing punches, scratching and swearing, the witch kept speaking, first in a whisper and then loudly, so loud the sound of the magic words filled my ears. I could hear nothing else. Now the enchantments were not falling off me as they should. No, they stuck to my skin like living ribbons. The enchantments wrapped around my arm and neck and began to tighten.

Finally able to best me, at least for the moment, Nemesis dragged me to the front of the store and shoved my face on the dirty screen. "Can't stop looking at yourself, can you? Your pride has always been your downfall, Ra-ma-ra. You could have been so much more—even a god—but you could not tear yourself away from your own face and figure. So much like Narcissus."

Her words filled me with rage, and I forced my eyes closed. "Witch!" I yelled like a madman. "When I get out of here, I am coming for you." She didn't care; my threat didn't scare her one bit until a cop car pulled into the driveway with lights flashing and sirens blaring. She slammed my head on the counter, and I shoved my elbow into her gut. Her black wings wrapped around me like she wanted to hide me from the cop, but I tore at them with my free hand. She screamed in pain and fell to the ground. At the same time, the witch dropped her enchantments and slipped out of the back of the store.

I could feel her leave, feel the magic fade and disappear. All that was left in the store was Nemesis and me. She had a bloody lip and a bruise on her face. I could have sworn it hadn't been there a minute ago. Her wings had vanished, and she clutched her arm with a smile. All around her were hundreds of broken bottles. The floor looked like a sea of red wine.

Running through the open door was the cop, the one I'd met earlier. The one who loved Thessalonike. He saw me right away, and Nemesis called to him, "Cruise! Look out! He's got a knife!"

"What?" I shouted. "She's lying." Before I could say another word, the idiot shot his primitive weapon at me. The barbs pierced my skin, and before I could say "Nemesis," lightning shot through me. No—it was electricity.

The damn fool tased me.

I was really starting not to like this guy.

Chapter
Thirteen—Cruise

Crisis Management

"On the floor, dude. You stay on the floor." I shouted at the tall man who was now covered in glass and blood. He'd torn up Fred's store, and I had a sneaking suspicion that Fred had left this world for the next. Lucy was crying now. I didn't think I had ever seen her cry the entire time I had known her. "Stay where you are, Lucy. I've got help on the way."

Her tears stopped immediately. "Who's coming? Belloc?"

"Chief Belloc," I spoke into my radio. "What's your ETA?"

"Don't call him. I'm fine. Look. I'm standing up now, see?" I could hardly believe it. Except for the busted lip and the bruised cheek, she didn't have but a few scratches on her. She dusted the glass off her blue jean shorts like it was sand and wiped away the tears.

"Stay where you are, Lucy."

"That's not Lucy, idiot," the man said, looking as pissed off as I felt. What the hell was wrong with the people on this island? Why was everyone losing their minds? Full moon? Too much fun at the Mullet Toss? I couldn't figure it. Suddenly, there was a funny smell. Like wet dog but worse. Looking down at the man I had in handcuffs (somehow that happened), I sniffed. No. It wasn't him, but he did smell different—like a cross between an orange and Christmas tinsel. Now *I* was losing my mind!

"Lucy, Chief Belloc is on the way." I struggled to help Ray or whatever this guy's name was off the floor. "Stop walking around the crime scene. In fact, go out the front door as slowly as you can."

All of a sudden I heard this monstrous unfolding, rustling sound, and the foul smell was overpowering now. I began to turn slowly to face the danger, but I caught a glimpse in the television monitor. A black-skinned creature with feathered legs and a woman's face was standing behind me. Lucy stood behind it, and she'd changed too. Lucy had wings! Wings like an ibis! What the hell was wrong with me?

"Run!" Ray yelled at me. I snatched him up from the ground to get him on his feet, and I took off behind him to the door.

"Where are *you* going? Someone wants to meet you. Someone very special." The creature—no, a harpy, I somehow knew that was what it was—had black fingernails and a black tongue. It didn't mind showing me either of them. I couldn't use my Taser; I had already deployed it on Ray. I reached for my pistol instead. The harpy waved its finger at me and quick as lightning snatched the gun from my hand. It clamped its hand over my mouth and whispered something in my ear. Sounded like, "Shifter blood in you."

"Shut up and put him in the back of the truck. The other stupid cop will be here before you know it." The harpy tilted its head back, its breasts fully exposed now, and let out a scream like a wildcat. I had to be hallucinating. Yeah, that was it. Lloyd had been poisoned, and I had sipped that poison too. Maybe I hadn't drunk enough to die, just enough to destroy my brain. And to think, I thought Lucy liked me.

Just then, Lucy smiled at me. Maybe she was hearing my thoughts right now. What in the world was happening? Her smile faded. No longer amused, she hit me over the head with a bottle. I felt something split and then passed out.

When I woke up, the harpy was gone. It was just Lucy and me sitting in the barroom. I was tied to a chair, and all the lights in the Pirateer were off. I would have thought everything was normal if the jukebox had been blaring Bad Moon Rising like it normally did at least ten times a night. But nope. I was tied to the rickety bamboo chair, and a few candles on the bar gave the only light in the room. "Ow, what did you hit me for, Lucy? I thought we were friends!"

The woman turned around, and she wasn't Lucy. No, this woman was taller than Lucy—and taller than me, for that matter. She was what I'd heard described as willowy, tall and thin with just enough curves to make her feminine. She was runway model beautiful, with shiny dark hair and even shinier eyes. Before she spoke I knew she was intelligent. Smarter than me. And I was tied to a chair. Did I mention that?

"What am I doing here? I am Officer Cruise Castille, and I am placing you under arrest. Untie me right now."

She did not smile but merely appraised me as if she were trying to determine if I was brave or just plain dumb. I'd settle for dumb. The sooner I could get away from her, the better. She gave off a creepy vibe.

"Where is Lucy? And Ray?" I asked, trying to keep my voice level.

"I am Roxana, the wife of Alexander the Great. Does that shock you?" She leaned on her elbows and cupped her chin in her hands. She had a seductive voice and penetrating eyes.

"And I'm the King of England. Now, what do you want?"

"It would do me no good to tell you what I want. You could not give it to me even if you lived a thousand lifetimes."

My head was pounding, and I wasn't feeling generous. "Well, then why am I here?"

"Good question, Officer Castille. You are here as bait."

"Bait for what? Like shark bait?"

"What I intend to catch does sometimes swim in the water. You know her as Thessalonike, the girl who owns a souvenir shop, but she's so much more. I wonder, would you be willing to set your belief system aside for a few minutes? Are you too closed minded to see the truth I am about to show you?" She pulled a knife out and laid it on the bar.

"And what's that for?"

"That is for a test, Castille. Castille—you must have some Spanish blood in there somewhere. Do you know if you do?"

"You dragged me here to talk to me about my genealogy?"

She sighed and rolled her eyes. "I see you aren't going to make this fun at all, so here goes. Thessalonike is a siren. She is the sister of my husband, Alexander. I need her blood to resurrect him and open the Sirens Gate. The gate will make my greatest wish come true. You know what I wish more than anything?"

"I am going to say your biggest wish is to rule the world." I quietly worked at the ropes that secured me to the chair.

"Well, yes and no. I could care less about the world, but Alexander is destined to rule. No matter what lifetime he incarnates. He is the King of the Civilized World. And I am his queen."

"Sounds like you have it all worked out. What do you need me for?"

"I need her blood. It is his blood. Isn't that something? I love this whole DNA thing. I need her to come rescue you. So here's what I am going to do. I am going to send her a body part of yours and see if I can get her attention. She's got that crazy angel with her, but then you've met him. So what do you think? Do they have something going on together or what?"

"Body part? Hold on, lady. I'm an officer of the law. Do you know what will happen to you if you hurt me? They will put you under the jail."

"No, can't do that. There's already somebody under the jail. She's sleeping, and if I were you, I wouldn't wake her up. You would be just her type."

My head swam, and I couldn't stand the crazy sound of her laugh. The feeling that I was in some sort of nightmare grew and grew. "Wake up, Cruise. Time to get up," I whispered to myself.

"Yes, wake up, Cruise. Let's all wake up." She showed me the knife. She stood an inch from my face and stared at me. Her dark brown eyes seemed animalistic. She sniffed me.

"Supernatural blood, and you don't even know it. That's rich. Did she never tell you? What a friend she is! Well, now I don't feel so bad about cutting you; it's just going to grow back. Since you're a newbie at this, I will cut something small. What about your...finger?"

"No! Come on, lady! Queen, um, Roxana! Please don't cut me. I need that finger. I am sure I can call her on the phone. Nobody needs to have their body parts removed." A harpy, probably the same one from earlier, came into the room. The evil thing clapped its hands and stuck its tongue out at me.

"Fine, we will try it your way, but I'm not ruling out dismemberment. I am giving you this one chance." Waving her knife around, Roxana pushed the phone toward me and as quick as lightning untied me. "Now call her and don't do anything stupid."

"Got it." I dialed with shaking fingers. Nik was right. She'd been right the whole time. It was complicated. And she was right about another thing too. I wouldn't understand.

What the hell had I gotten myself into?

I wanted to cry when she picked up. Instead, I took a deep breath and said, "Hey, Nik. This is Cruise. Listen, I am down here at the Pirateer with a few of your friends, and they want to cut off my finger. Something about Alexander the Great, the gate and the queen. Can you come here?"

The queen interjected, "No, not here. Tell her to meet us at the gate. We must all be together to open it."

"Oh, never mind. The queen says that she wants you to meet us at the gate. That we must all be together to open it. Do you know what that means?"

Nik's voice was calm. It would have been eerie except for all the bizarre things I'd seen today. "Cruise, listen very carefully. Don't be a hero. Do what you are told, okay? Just forget all those action movies. This isn't the time. I will meet you at the gate. We will all be there. But please, stay alive. Don't make her mad, Cruise. Okay?" Before I could answer, Roxana hung up the phone.

"Good job. And she is correct. You don't want to make me angry, boy. Now we wait for nightfall and then leave for the gate. I wonder what mischief we can get into before then."

The harpy winked at me, but Lucy looked tired and angry. She sulked at me, but I had no idea why. I was the one being held prisoner here. Not her. None of them spoke, and I didn't say anything else either. Better to keep my mouth shut, although I had my cell phone in my pocket. What were the chances I could get it and call the chief?

Roxana walked to a booth and curled up with a package of silk. The harpy, seeing I was more interested in Lucy, and that no blood would be spilled, transformed into a rather plain woman. She stuck out her tongue at me and stood over the jukebox, just flipping through the records. Lucy stood beside me. "Now you know it all. You know why I was glad it wasn't you. I had to do it, but I didn't want to. I told her that, but she didn't listen to me."

"I see. So you thought you'd kill Lloyd instead."

"I don't love you, Cruise. Never have. You were a means to an end. I want Ramara, but I lost him. I want him back. I need her dead and out of the way. Then I can claim what is mine."

"You talking about Nik? I happen to care about her. Like I used to care about you."

She looked away for a moment. "That's nice to know. It's been a long time since anyone cared about me. Of course I might actually believe you if your life wasn't in my hands at the moment."

"Whatever. You tried to kill me, Lucy. I think that might be considered a friendship killer."

"You have no idea what I'm capable of," she said with a smile, her sultry voice in my ear. "If I wanted you dead, you would be dead."

Before I could answer, my phone rang in my pocket. Every "woman" in the bar was on me then, digging in my pants. It wasn't exciting at all. "Who is it?" Roxana asked.

"It's someone named Belloc," the harpy said, squinting at my phone.

"That's his boss. Answer it."

The harpy, Desiree was the name I heard Lucy call her, said in a bubbly voice, "Hey, this is Desiree. Lucy wants to talk to you."

"Yeah, we have him. He's at the bar. Mmm hmmm. Yes. Okay, we'll see you there."

"This just gets better and better," I moaned. Now my boss was involved with these crazies?

"Hey, your head is bleeding. I can doctor that."

"No thanks, Lucy. I would rather bleed to death."

"Fine by me. Just do me a favor. Bleed slowly because we need you alive when we take you to the gate."

Chapter Fourteen—Nike

Plans Change

Plans Change

Plans Change I should have stayed asleep. These two were intolerable. Ramara showed up at my house with Agrios, and he looked as if he'd fallen into a vat of razor blades. Unwilling to be attended by anyone, he was in my bathroom rummaging through my first aid kit while I sorted out the latest domestic dispute. So much for supernatural healing. Too bad he didn't have his necklace. He was a mess, and I had no clear picture as to why yet.

Heliope was not amused by Agrios' appearance. Neither was I, actually, but there had to be a reason why Ramara had brought him here. Heliope screeched at him as he tried to hug her. "I'm not taking you back, you dirty old man." Then she turned to me. "Why is he here? What have I done to make you hate me enough to drag this thing up?"

"Hey! We need allies. Meri brought him here for a reason." My heart hurt at saying her name. I had gone looking for her, but the mermaid was nowhere to be found. Perhaps she had enough sense to make herself scarce while all this went down, but I kind of doubted it. I had never known Meri to back down from a fight, even with Roxana. Even to her own detriment.

"I don't want his help. Get your filthy hands off of me!" She picked up a glass decanter and slung it at him. He gracefully ducked but didn't seem to get the hint.

"Please let the anger go, wife. This was so long ago, and you know you alone will always hold my heart." Agrios turned on the charm now, but Heliope wasn't having any of it.

"Why would I want that booze-soaked organ?" she yelled, looking for something else to pitch his way.

In typical Agrios fashion, he misinterpreted her comment as an invitation. "Then what other organ would you like to possess, my dear?"

Standing upright like one of the statues of her that used to line the walkways of her ancient temple, she brooded with anger. "How about your tongue? Or your eyes! Is that an organ? I think that would be a proper offering! I am sick of looking at you. I am going to end this right now!" I saw her hand rise as if she were ready to cast him a blow; I had to intervene. If I let this go on too much longer, there would be an all-out war of the gods happening right here on Dauphin Island. So much for anonymity.

"You two cut it out right now, or I'm going to drown you both myself!" I didn't know what came over me, but they shut up at least for the moment. "Here's how this is going to go—no more fighting until Roxana has been defeated and the gate is secure. No more breaking things in my house!" That comment I directed to my stepmother. And then I wheeled around toward Agrios. "And you! No more trying to sex up everything that walks. If you are not willing to help us, Meri can take you back right now. We have enough to worry about besides you!"

About that time my cell phone rang. I pulled it out of my pocket and stared at the screen. It was Cruise again, calling from his cell and not the Pirateer. I wondered what else he had to tell me about Roxana. "Cruise, are you okay? You didn't try to be a hero, did you?"

"Hello, pretty girl." Feeling frozen to the spot, I tapped on the screen to put her on speaker phone. It was Roxana. This wasn't good. Not at all.

"Where is he?"

Heliope listened carefully; Agrios sat on the bed and watched me pace around the room.

Roxana said in a sick-sweet voice, "Cruise? Say hi, sweetie."

He came on the line, and his voice was shaking a bit. "Hey, Nik. Sorry about this."

"No, it's fine. Did she change her plan? Are you...okay?" I chewed my fingernail nervously as I listened to him. He was in pain, but he was as calm as could be expected.

"Don't do anything foolish. Don't listen to her, Nik. She's got—"

I listened in horror to the sounds of a struggle.

I screamed into the phone as Ramara came and stood behind me. "No! You bitch! Don't you touch him!"

"Aw, so sad, pretty girl. Listen to me, and he will live. Don't listen to me, and he will die. Meet at the gate at sunset."

"I got the message the first time, sister."

"I wanted to make sure you were actually coming. I grow anxious to hold my husband again. Come alone. Make peace with whatever god you serve, Thessalonike, for tonight your blood is required. I will exchange your life for his. That is the deal."

Heliope shook her head, but I did not pay any attention to her. I closed my eyes and agreed. "I will be there at sunset. Alone. But if you harm one hair on his head, I will hurt you in ways you could only imagine."

"Oh, now you are speaking my language. See you then." She hung up, and I was left to stare at the blank screen.

"Why did you let her take Cruise? Didn't you think keeping him safe was important?" I railed at Ramara.

"Don't take it out on me, and no I didn't think it all that important. He is not on my task list. Protect you, protect the gate. Those are the wishes of the Order. I care nothing about this man."

"Well, I do, you rotten bastard. You were going to let him die!"

"The chances are good that he will die regardless of whether I help him or not. We cannot trade you, no matter what. That idea is off the table; I can see it running through your mind, princess, but we cannot do that."

"You don't decide what's off the table, eloi!"

"Stop this!" Agrios commanded. It was his turn to pace my bedroom now. "This is some kind of witchcraft that has us all arguing! Are there witches nearby?"

"In fact, there are, and there's one other thing." We waited to hear what the one other thing was. Ramara lowered his voice. "Nemesis is here, and she's helping Roxana. The police officer called her Lucy."

Lucy was Nemesis? Now my head was really spinning.

"What have I gotten myself into here?" Agrios wiped his lips with the back of his hand; his eyes were red. "Do you have any wine? I think better when I have wine, and I am going to need it."

I shook my head. "No, she drank it all." Heliope looked at her sandaled toe but otherwise didn't seem the least bit embarrassed by all this. "I think I might have some beer in the refrigerator. I guess the liquor store is out of the question?"

Ramara nodded, "Definitely. I'll get the beer. It will have to do."

"Very well, for now. Where can we sit together?"

"In the kitchen. Come on. First let me take care of any curse that might be hanging around. And there's no telling who's listening, either." I flipped the dial on the small transistor radio and tuned in to a vibrant jazz station. I could pick up only a few stations out this far, and this was my favorite. Music, especially instrumental music, provided relief from curses—at least some of them.

Ramara paused as he leaned into the refrigerator looking for the lone bottle of beer I had stashed there. I could see by his tense jawline he was also mentally scanning the area outside, a special skill that only angels of his kind had. I had this skill to a limited degree, but mine was always more accurate in the water. "No one is here. Not yet. Won't be long, though." He popped the top on the beer with his bare hand and set the bottle down in front of Agrios. Agrios stared up at him as if he'd committed some major crime. Ramara waved his arms in frustration.

"I'll handle this. Honestly, you are being ridiculous, Agrios." I opened the cabinet and retrieved a beer glass for him. He sneered at the plain glass but poured the drink, watched it foam and then took a big swig.

"Oh, that's horrible. But any port in a storm." Heliope snorted at his comment but said nothing. She cocked her arm back over the chair and watched us, the anger still flickering in her eyes.

"We have only a short time, so let's work the details out," Agrios said with a smile as he rubbed his hands together.

"Why are you so gung-ho now?" I asked him suspiciously. No way would I ever trust this man...god...thing. Whatever he was or thought himself to be. "Just a short time ago you were looking for the exit. Now you want to lead the charge?"

"That was before he knew Nemesis was involved." He gestured toward Ramara, who crinkled at hearing her name but kept his mouth shut.

"That matters to you?" I asked Agrios, still unsure.

"It should matter to us all, Thessalonike. If Nemesis is on this island, she had to have broken free from her prison to get here. I know for a fact she was imprisoned. I stood as one of the judges at her trial."

"You mean like you were imprisoned?" Heliope questioned him as she took a sip of his beer.

"No, not like I was. I wasn't imprisoned, only detained on a veiled island. She was in the place Under the Earth." Collectively we shivered. Although I had no clear understanding of what the phrase actually meant, I knew it was not a place I wanted to visit. "Her escape can mean only one thing: the Order has lost its power to confine. If that is the case, then we have bigger problems than Roxana and Nemesis to worry about. This is bigger than that." He lifted the glass and drained it. "Tell me, eloi, what have you seen?"

I noticed Ramara didn't correct Agrios over what he called him. He related what he'd told me earlier about Faydra, and we all mentioned things we'd seen. Things that weren't right. We were cast-off beings in an ever-changing world, but now the change had escalated in new and dangerous ways.

The screech of police cars slinging gravel in my driveway brought the conversation to a halt. This wasn't just the Podunk local cops. These were county police cars, four of them, with probably more on the way. Chief Belloc stepped out of his car with a bullhorn. "Attention in the house. This is the Dauphin Island Police Department. We have the house surrounded—come out with your hands up. You have sixty seconds to comply."

"What the hell?" I whispered. "I thought we had until sunset. No way is this a coincidence."

"Roxana must know I'm here. They want to make sure you don't escape."

Heliope stood in front of me as if to shield me. "We need to get you out of here now."

"To where? They say we're surrounded!"

Ramara and Agrios exchanged glances, and the bad feeling I had a minute ago returned. "Which one you want?" Ramara asked.

"I'll take the front." Agrios' grin had disappeared, and he licked his lips thirstily. I wondered how much good he was going to be in this fight. What was the advantage of having a booze-powered being on your side if he had no booze?

"Hold on a second." I sprinted across the room and slung open the half-size Tiki bar.

"For god's sake, Nik, we don't have time for this!" Ramara growled at me.

I didn't remind him that only my friends called me that. He was risking his life to save mine. Didn't that make him my friend? "Got it!" I pitched two small bottles of whiskey to Agrios, who immediately began cracking them open.

"Oh, that's awful. Thank you! I'm ready!"

"Time is not on our side! Agrios, don't kill anyone if you don't need to. Get free from the officers and meet us at the gate. Sun won't be down for a little while. Nik, if you have to hide...where should we meet?"

I ignored Chief Belloc and his bullhorn as he began a countdown like we were about to blow out some candles or something. He even sounded happy about it. "Let's meet at the town clock. It's at the East End before you get to the fort. There are some pavilions, but beyond that is a concrete tunnel. We can meet there. Okay?"

"Right. Follow me. Take my hand; I'll cover you." Without waiting for permission, he grabbed my hand and practically dragged me to the back door.

"I don't need you to cover me. I think I've got this under control, Ramara." The idea was to give a quick blast or two of song, but before I could vocalize the sounds, bullets began flying. Agrios started to laugh stupidly. He grabbed Heliope and kissed her before he shoved her to the side and walked to the front door.

"I'm coming out!"

"Where's the girl?" Belloc called to him as we flew out the back. Ramara's enchantment covered us, hiding us from the human cops who flanked my house.

"I've got her here. She's coming out with me!"

The three of us ran for the neighbor's backyard and kept running until we were at the corner of Cadillac and Lemoyne. We had about a half mile more to go, but we had to run across traffic to get to the other side of the highway. "Screw this. Let's swim."

"Damn. This is going to mess up my hair," Heliope complained, but she was the first in the water. We slid in without drawing any attention. Meri appeared and took my hand with a smile. I squeezed her hand, and together we swam through the small harbor to the other side of the island. With each kick of my feet, I thought about Cruise and what he might be going through. How could I leave him to deal with Roxana on his own?

I wasn't. I couldn't. And I wasn't going to wait until tonight, either. As Ramara and Heliope swam ahead of us, I tugged on Meri's hand, compelling her to slow her pace.

We must go find Cruise, Meri. He was at the Pirateer. Do you know if he's still there?

She paused and frowned at me. She sent me a wave of fear, but I shook my head.

No fear for me. Cruise needs me. Where is he? She put her hands on her hips and tilted her head. It was a funny sight considering she had barely any hips to speak of and no feet. Any other time, I would have been rolling with laughter.

Please, Meri. I have to help him or she'll kill him.

She sent me waves of love and with an expressive wave told me to follow her. In a minute we were at the shore behind the Pirateer. Bobbing my head up from the water, I could see an open back door.

I didn't have a plan, but I had a burning desire to rescue Cruise. He deserved better than this.

You protect from here, okay? Meri gripped my forearms and shook her head furiously. She was going to make this difficult. I knew it was crazy and reckless, but I had to take the chance. He would do the same for me.

I hugged her and pushed away to climb onshore. At least the beach was steep and I couldn't be easily seen from the bar. I squeezed the water from my hair as I crept up the side of a log of driftwood.

I heard the sound of screaming coming from the open door of the Pirateer.

It was Cruise.

Chapter Fifteen—Nike

Violent Urge

I heard Meri splash behind me, and I waved my hand at her without looking back. Our movements had to be limited, but it wasn't likely that we were going to get the jump on Roxana. Unless we were lucky. If Meri wasn't more careful, she'd give away my position; the element of surprise was about the only thing I had going for me. I became aware that someone was on the other side of the log shimmying up the beach with me. I turned my head slightly.

Ramara! He rolled his eyes at me to let me know I had his full disapproval, but his tattoos glowed slightly. He must have felt excited about the impending fight. Eloi and sirens didn't communicate telepathically, except in extreme circumstances, but I didn't need that to know he wasn't happy with me in the least. Well, if he was going to be my friend, he'd have to get used to that. I was an impetuous woman. Ramara stifled a groan and pounded his fists in the sand. This was more than impatience with me—he was in pain.

"What is it?" I whispered.

"The Order calls me to the gate." So the Order had abandoned me. Whatever. When had they ever helped me?

I didn't know what to do, how to help him. "Then go. I'll get Cruise." I scrambled up a few more feet as sand stuck to my damp body.

Ramara hung back slightly for another minute, but he appeared to get a grip on the pain. When he reached the top of the beach, he nodded toward the bar, asking me to take the lead. *This was my idea, wasn't it? So what was my idea?* A beer truck rumbled into the back parking lot; I watched the driver roll to a stop, blocking the doorway and our view inside. Great.

"Hey, can you tell where they are?" I whispered to Ramara.

"If I use my powers, she will know I am here." He was talking about Nemesis. He'd been intimate with her, and because of her nature, she would always have a general idea of where he was. Someone from the bar walked outside, and I heard the jukebox cranking Creedence Clearwater Revival's *Suzie Q.*

"No deliveries today, Bill. Come back tomorrow."

"What?" The young man with the red hat jumped out of the truck. "You can't just refuse a delivery, Lucy. I have other places to be." He clearly didn't realize that he took his life in his hands. Talk about being in the wrong place at the wrong time.

"You'll just have to deal with it. We've got freezer problems, and I can't accept the delivery. Come back tomorrow. I can accept the order then."

Fortunately, Bill wouldn't take no for an answer. I walked as lightly as I could up the small hill and scrambled to the truck. I stood by the rear tire on the passenger side. Ramara hissed at me, but I didn't listen to or look at him.

I couldn't see Lucy—Nemesis—but I felt her pause. The tone of her voice changed too. "You know what? I don't have time to argue with you, Bill. Put the beer in the closet over there. I'll have one of my guys move it later."

"Really? That doesn't look too secure. You'll have to sign to show you're responsible." She muttered something under her breath, but I could hear the pen scratch across the paper. Bill must have gotten the message, because he rolled up his truck's rear door and began wheeling out beer as he whistled victoriously.

A few minutes later, the truck rolled slowly away and I walked beside the rear tire, hopefully hidden from the view of the supes inside.

So now what, Thessalonike? You managed to sneak to the front of the bar. Is that so amazing?

I hid behind the oversize pirate statue outside the front door. I tried to get the lay of the land through the colored glass window, but I couldn't see a thing except distorted light from a few candles. Carefully, I tugged on the door, and to my surprise it opened. Taking a deep breath, I slid inside the dank foyer of the dim bar and stood flattened against the wall. For the second time today, I wished I could send Ramara a message telepathically. Maybe I could, but I wasn't willing to risk it. Not with Cruise yelling in pain. Or was that anger?

"I told you I'm a law enforcement officer. Do you realize the consequences of hurting me?"

"I can't tell you how impressed I am," a woman purred.

Now what? I had two choices. Wait to be discovered or bust into the bar. I was opting for choice two when I heard a loud thud on the roof above me. I knew right away it was Ramara. He stomped across the roof five or six times, and that was all it took. Following the voices, he walked toward the back of the bar, giving me the perfect cover to step inside unseen.

Pushing the door open slightly, I slipped in and fell to my knees to avoid being seen. Cruise sat at the bar, tied to a rickety old barstool. Nemesis and Roxana were nowhere to be found, but a short, black-haired woman with no rhythm stood in front of the jukebox dancing—if you could call it that—and smoking a cigarette. She had her back to me as she scanned through the music and dropped in a few more quarters. I poked Cruise on the leg, and he kicked instinctively. His lip was busted, and he had a large handprint bruise on his face. I could see blood on his hands too. I put my finger over my lips and tugged at the rope with shaking fingers.

"Suzie Q, baby, I love you, Suzie Q." The strange woman sang as well as she danced, but as long as she was busy, I was okay with that.

Whoever tied the knots knew what they were doing. Ramara continued to stomp around on the roof, and I frantically worked with the rope until I heard a voice behind me say, "Well, well, well. Look what the cat dragged in." Roxana. Before I could get on my feet, she kicked me, nailing me in the shoulder. I toppled over and knocked Cruise to the ground. He landed with a loud thud and a groan, but I couldn't help him. The crazy dancer had half-transformed into a harpy with dangerous black claws. It scratched at me and began to screech, letting the others know I was present.

I felt my powers begin to awaken. "Cover your ears, Cruise!"

"I can't! I'm still tied to this damn—okay, never mind. I'm loose."

"Cover them now!" The harpy charged at me, and I stood up.

I opened my mouth, and divine music began to fill it. I tilted back my head and sang as loudly as I could. Nobody here would understand the words, except Roxana, for it was in a language long dead to the world. After just a few notes, the harpy was screaming with her hands over her ears. I kept singing. It was a love song, an ancient one about Lorelei, a siren who lived across the sea and waited for her human lover.

As I sang my tune, the harpy began to shake and blood poured out of its ears. It crawled toward the door, its powers waning; soon it was once again just a plain old redneck woman wearing blue jeans that were too big for her and a tank top. As a siren, it wasn't in my nature to kill, despite what the fairy tales said. Sirens loved, and rages hated. It was dangerous for me to hate too long. I could flip, and I had before, but I always flipped back. Once, I got dangerously close...

"Help me, Nik." Cruise's voice sounded weak. I let the harpy go and went to him. He must have heard a few of the notes, because his nose was bleeding.

"Did I do that?"

"No, it was already like that thanks to Lucy. And I think I cracked a rib or something. I can't get up."

"Use your phone and call 911. Can you do that? I have to go to the gate. I have to stop Roxana."

"What the hell is going on, Nik? I hear you are some kind of mermaid or something? Is this true or did she poison me? I have to be hallucinating, right?"

"I'll explain it all to you soon. For now, lie here and call 911. Have them take you to the hospital. I'll come find you when this is done. I promise."

I stood up to leave, fighting the urge to cradle him in my arms and hold him until help arrived. Maybe Ramara could heal him? Did I want to do that, though? I stared at his abdomen with my siren's gaze. He was right, he did have a cracked rib and some nasty internal bleeding. "Tell them you have a cracked rib and some internal bleeding. You're going to be all right. I have to go. I have to do this, Cruise. This is who I am."

"Okay, but I want to hear everything. Don't leave out a single detail!"

"Sure," I lied to him. I had no intention of giving him details. I would find a way to mesmerize him. He didn't need this kind of knowledge in his head. Knowing too much would put him in more danger than he already was.

"Wait!" he yelled at me. "One more thing."

"What is it?"

"Is this a date? I mean, we've been in a bar fight together. So the next date would be date two, right?"

"Cruise..."

"Just humor, Nik. I did take an ass-beating for you."

"Okay, the next date will be our second date. Are you happy?"

"Yep," he said with a goofy grin. I rolled my eyes at him. It was kind of an inside joke we'd had going for a while. We'd been debating when it was appropriate to sleep with someone you'd been dating. He said three dates, and I said four. I guess he was hoping we'd "hook up" on our third date, but he had a surprise coming. Even though I was older than all the women on this island put together—well, human women—I just wasn't that kind of gal. But I'd let him believe it. For the moment.

I ran out of the bar as he called 911 with a bloody smile. That harpy wasn't coming back. It had gotten its ass kicked and would be licking its wounds for a while. I wouldn't be surprised if it was gone off the island by now. Harpies were cowards, and even the smallest scratch freaked them out.

I had to help Ramara, but the eloi was gone. So were Nemesis and Roxana. I knew where they were headed. I had to get there. Now!

Chapter Sixteen—Nike

The Mermaid's Gift

I decided to steal Cruise's car to get to the gate quickly. Strangely, there wasn't even one light glowing on the island. It was like the whole darn place had lost power. Maybe the Order was trying to help us after all. It was worth a shot, wasn't it?

If I knew the supernaturals, they wouldn't be concerned about a human vehicle. Hey, it was the best idea I could come up with right now. During my time in the bar, the sun had gone down and a few early stars had appeared.

Very soon, the gate, merely a rocky arch formation, would begin to glow with power. In ancient times, the gods and goddesses traveled around the world using these portals. That was why in some cultures people knew Ares and Hermes. Others called them other names, depending on the people who lived by those gates.

This was the last gate. It was connected to our original home in ancient Macedonia, but that wasn't its real power now. It was a power source. Period. Roxana, my sister-in-law, had used another gate to resurrect Alexander once before, but my brother had come back to us mad and raving.

Right before he sipped the Immortal Waters, I stole them and dumped them into the sea. I thought that was all of it, but apparently Roxana had kept some hidden. Without his immortality, Alexander had been easy to kill, but I didn't want to think about that now. The

Alexander I knew and loved had been long dead. He could never return to us. I would not allow it because I loved him.

As I got out of the car, I peered into the darkness. Something wasn't right. I heard a woman wailing—it was Roxana. Instead of sneaking down to the gate, I practically ran. Something was truly wrong—the gate was missing. What the heck? I couldn't believe what I was seeing.

Then falling through the sky like two flaming stars were Nemesis and Ramara, locked together in battle. Ramara's wings were fully extended, and I could see that Nemesis had a broken wing. She screeched in agony as Ramara roared at her. They tumbled from the sky to the sand and continued to wrestle. I watched as Nemesis grew very still; even her eyes were closed. I could see her face plainly in the moonlight.

"She's not dead!" I yelled, drawing attention to myself. Roxana flew at me, leaving Alexander's bones behind. Her natural beauty had hardened and her long dark hair was tucked behind her pointed ears, further proof that she was in full rage mode now. While sirens were creatures who used love as their defense, rages used hate. I could see the hate in her eyes now. They glowed green slightly, then purple.

"Where is the gate, Thessalonike? What have you done?" She hunched over and let out a scream like I had never heard. "I hate you for what you've done to Alexander. I hate you for what you have done to me! You will pay, pretty girl."

I leaped into the water, not to retreat but to show her I was ready for the fight. She dove in after me. I saw Meri creeping ever closer to Alexander's bones. She smiled and sent me waves of love.

As she disappeared quickly into the down deep, Roxana and I stood on the churning Gulf waters and began to do battle. She shaped waves with her hands and sent them sloshing over me. I did the same, and for a while we traded water attacks until we were both soaked.

"Enough of this!" Roxana began to spin on the water, faster and faster until it became clear what she was attempting to do. She was using dark water magic. If she could wrap me in her dark waters, she would simply spin me into oblivion. This was powerful magic, more powerful than mine. Thankfully I felt waves of love wash over me. Meri's pale face popped up behind Roxana, and she continued to send her waves until the rage caught her. Roxana sent a blast of blue energy but missed Meri completely.

The only way I could get rid of her or make her lose her focus was to distract her from her current rageful purpose. "Did you lose something, Roxana? I don't see that bag you were carrying. You sure you brought it with you?" I knew my mesmerizing eyes were glowing blue now. Roxana cast her eyes on the shore but did not see the bag.

"Alexander! Where are you?" As if he could answer.

"He's dead, Roxana. He's been dead. Don't bring him back, or he'll die again."

I overplayed my hand because the rage hit me with a blue flame that temporarily muted me. Then I felt Meri's waves again, healing waves of love and peace. I felt better, but I was not fully recovered yet.

Roxana's hands began to glow blue again, but I wasn't focused on her. A flying being was approaching behind her, and she had not yet sensed him. It was Agrios. I kept my face like stone as he approached. He scooped his arms under hers and carried her away, using a binding spell to keep her mute and calm. I assumed he was trying to take her to the closest veiled island, but I could have been mistaken. What I knew about Agrios could fit in a wine glass. He must have found some of that because he seemed pretty happy as he tried to fly away, but Roxana broke free again and fell into the water and disappeared.

Where was Heliope, the goddess who had pledged to protect me? Nowhere to be found. *Heliope, I summon you*, I whispered. *Where are you?*

As I sat catching my breath. I waited for an answer. I heard a faint whisper: *I am here. Watch yourself, Thessalonike.* Immediately I stood and looked for the danger.

Nemesis was now standing over Ramara as if she had beaten him. In her hand she held a necklace. Ramara's healing necklace! The one his father had given him—the one she had stolen from him. Would she now taunt him with it?

"No, Nemesis! You don't know what you are doing!" Ramara shouted.

"I call on the power of this necklace. I command it to work for me." Instead of seeing a power activate, Nemesis watched in surprise as lighting hit the water—and it was coming closer. Without knowing it, she had summoned Ramara's father to fight for him.

"I told you it wouldn't work for you. Give it to me, Nemesis, before he kills you. My father is Poseidon. He won't show you any mercy."

Still thinking this was a game, unwilling to admit defeat, she dangled the necklace over him as he lay halfway in the water. Suddenly, Meri jumped out of the water like a dolphin and snatched the necklace from her hand. She sent waves of joy to me as she dove back into the shallow water and swam off. With her wings fully extended, Nemesis made her hands into two fists and punched them together. I saw Meri's body disappear under the water.

"Meri! No!" Meri appeared again, obviously wounded. There was a hole in her tail, and blood was pouring from the wound. Still, she clutched the necklace. Nemesis flew to her as Ramara called her back.

"Give me that, mermaid!" Nemesis tossed her wet, dark hair back and showed her pretty face. But she was so full of bitterness that it marred her beauty.

Meri was still in the shallows and struggling. Nemesis pounded her fists together again, but this time I leapt between them, taking the blow for my friend. Her power took my breath away, and my chest now had a hole in it. Could this be the end of me? Meri sent me love, but her healing waves were weak and not much help. "No, Meri. Heal yourself. I'll be okay. Friend is okay." Meri crawled up beside me, the necklace clutched in her hand. She was in only six inches of water, but she lay in my lap protectively. Her turquoise eyes were heartbroken as she sent more waves of love, regret and fear.

"No regret, no fear, Meri. All will be well," I cried as she lay unmoving in the water.

My friend was dead. She'd spent all her energy healing me, saving me. Now she was gone. She who had thought of nothing else but to love and serve me was gone. "No! No, Meri! Wake up!" Everyone got quiet. It was a rare thing to see a mermaid die. But the sanctity of the moment did not last long.

"Still want to play?" Nemesis taunted me, her eyes on the necklace.

I saw Agrios again. This time he wore a look of determination like I'd never seen. He scooped up Nemesis and carried her away. She was suddenly gone from the fight, but I was still full of rage. I was on the verge of crossing over. *Meri! How could I have done this to you!*

Ramara was there now speaking to me, but I could not hear him. All I could hear was the pounding of my own heart: *Hate, hate hate.*

Roxana was running toward me, and I began to scream with rage. She laughed at the sound.

Ramara shook me. "You are a siren! Not a rage! You can't do this! Roxana has lost, Thessalonike. Meri hid the bones. Roxana will never find them now. She cannot hurt you anymore."

He turned to her and shouted, "Go, Roxana! Go, and never come back here. Alexander is gone. You have no right to the gate. Hear now the proclamation of the Order. You are no longer fit to use the gate. You will not return here on pain of death. Go home to Greece and never return! What you want can never be."

Roxana began to wail and weep. She walked out into the ocean and kept walking and wailing until she was completely gone. Immediately, I went back to Meri and pulled her on to the shore. She was gone, but her sweet face was as lovely as it had always been.

"I am sorry about your friend," Ramara said, touching my shoulder lightly.

"She died trying to heal me. She did heal me. She sacrificed her own life for mine. How can I live with that?" Silver tears rolled out of my eyes. Those were the sign of a new, unexplored power. Ramara didn't miss them either. He picked up Meri and began to walk to the beach.

"What are you doing? Where are you taking her?"

"To the gate."

"There is no gate now. The Order must have destroyed it."

"No, it's here. Come out now, Heliope." The air began to shimmer, and soon I could see Heliope standing atop the rocks that made the Sirens Gate formation.

"Phew, I am exhausted. I can't believe how much work that took. I must be getting old."

"You did that?"

"Of course I did. Why do you doubt me, stepdaughter? I would never leave you to fight on your own. You are my charge, aren't you? Oh no. The mermaid. Such a sweet thing. What are you doing, Ramara?"

"I thought we'd see if this gate really worked. If the stars are right and there is enough power, maybe we can bring her back to life."

"How do we do it, then?" I asked.

Heliope gave me a small sad smile. "You can't. Only a god or goddess can initiate the gate. That's why Roxana called Nemesis to help her. Give her to me. I can walk through without being harmed. I don't know how long it will take for me to return. Sometimes it is right away, and other times it takes much longer. Sometimes it doesn't happen at all."

"This can't be goodbye," I said with tears in my eyes. "I can't say goodbye to you both, Heliope."

"You have a new protector now. He'll keep an eye on you for me." Ramara looked away, blushing. Heliope leaned toward me and said, "Just remember he's not as strong as he thinks."

"Hey, I heard that."

"Good, you were meant to. Remember your vow, sexy one." To me she said, "Take care of yourself, Thessalonike. There is much you have not remembered yet. I will be back as soon as I can. Tell Agrios..." She gave a wistful smile. "Well, they say that absence makes the heart grow fonder. Let's see if that is true."

Then she spoke the magic words and soon the gate was glowing bright purple. Ancient letters glowed in the rock arch. I read them quietly.

Oceans swell at the ringing of the bell at the Sirens Gate.

In a flash of purple light, Heliope and Meri disappeared. The Sirens Gate was once again just an interesting rock formation on Dauphin Island.

We sat in the sand, Ramara and I, staring at the ocean. Heliope and Meri were gone, hopefully alive somewhere. Agrios was headed to the veiled island with Nemesis (good riddance). Roxana had slipped away under the waves. Only Ramara and I were left.

"Where to now, my friend?"

"I've been thinking about that. I've been thinking about hanging around. Here, I mean. I wonder if this island could use another charter boat."

I punched his arm and smiled at him. "I'd like having you close."

"Really?" I smelled his excitement. He produced delicious pheromones when he was excited. I jumped up to my feet and wiped the sand off my clothing. Time to change the subject. I had Cruise to think about, and the honest truth was that Ramara wasn't over what happened with Nemesis. Not to mention that if he even kissed me, he'd lose his wings and become mortal. He was too proud for that. He might find me attractive, but he'd never love me like that.

But Cruise would. I wasn't sure that I loved him yet. Maybe I didn't, but I did want to see what happened. "Oh, by the way. This is yours." I handed him his necklace. "One last gift from Meri."

He accepted it with a smile and immediately put it on. Touching the pearl and gold pendant, he gave a nod of thanks. "She was the weakest of us all but the bravest. Minerva would be proud."

"Oh yes, Minerva. I expect we will be hearing from her."

"I expect so." We stood facing one another. We were so close now, I could feel the warmth of his skin. I could get lost in his scent, in his muscular....

"Whoa, Nik. We're friends. That's it."

I slapped his arm. "Oh my God! You mean you've been listening to my mind the whole time?"

"Well, not the *whole* time." He grinned like the mythological Cheshire cat.

"Ugh, I hate you." I turned to walk away.

"That's a lie. But don't worry, your secret is safe with me. I am still your protector."

I turned back and gave him a cautious smile. Then I left him there and went to find Cruise's car. I had somewhere else to be. Someone else I was supposed to be with.

This was the way it should be.

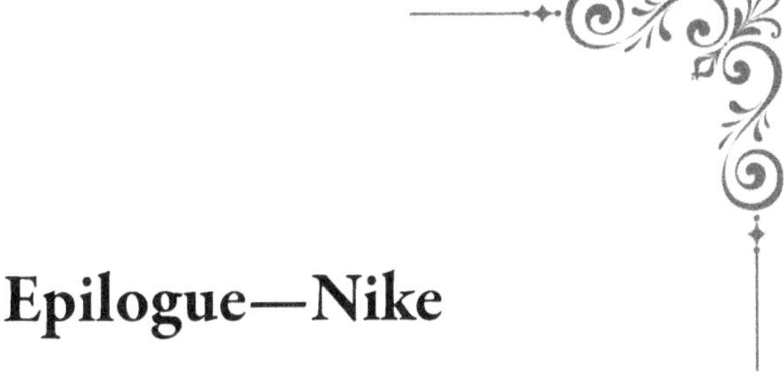

Epilogue—Nike

Sunshiny Day

S I walked into the police station with a picnic basket in my hand. "It's lunchtime, Officer Castille. I've got some fried fish and lots of goodies in here. Care to eat outside at the picnic table? It's a beautiful day."

"Why yes, I would love that. Molly, hold my calls please. Unless the District Attorney calls about Dan Belloc. I'm guessing he'll be gone for quite a while after all he's done." The older woman nodded.

"Imagine breaking into a liquor store. It's unheard of for a police chief." Cruise tidied up his desk, and I winked at Molly, who winked back. She was not only the secretary to the new chief of police but also the new Guardian of the Gate. I was glad she was there so I could finally leave that task to someone else. I was looking forward to traveling off the island. I had been here since the 1500s. It was time for a break.

"I had the weirdest dream last night, Nik. I dreamed about this thing...it had legs like a bird, a black bird, and the upper body of a woman. Anyway, it came after me. It had these black claws and a bird mouth. Ew...it was gross."

I plopped the basket down on the table and began removing the plastic containers. "Pizza dreams, probably," I offered disingenuously.

"Probably. It's just that I have dreamed it more than once. It bothers me. I know, I know, I am a grown man..."

"Stop that, Cruise. I am not making fun of you. Look at me. Everything is going to be all right."

"Will you stop that? Every time you say that, it gives me a headache."

"Sorry. You want a Coke?" I made a mental note to call Ramara. His mesmerizing power was greater than mine. Since Cruise had some supe blood; he needed someone stronger than me to make him forget. Ramara had done it once for me already, and I was sure I could talk him into doing it again.

"So, I've been thinking, Nik."

"Yes?" I said as I dug into the fruit salad.

"Technically this could be considered our second date."

"And your point?" I knew Cruise was a three-date kind of guy. He was young, handsome and eager to "get to know me better." That's the thing about mortals—they are always in a rush to see one another naked.

"No pressure, just wanted it on record."

"Listen, I'm a huge fan of spontaneity, Cruise. I hope that's okay."

"Well," he said, pretending to stroke his nonexistent beard, "can't I at least have a kiss?"

He closed his eyes and leaned close to me. I was tempted to lay one on him. It had been such a long time since I had given myself permission to let go of my inhibitions. I wasn't sure that the handsome young cop could curb my desire. I tapped his lip politely with the chastest of kisses and acted as innocently as I could. He seemed none the wiser. He grinned and kissed me quickly once more before changing the subject.

"So you do like me," he said confidently.

"Of course I like you. We've been friends for quite a while," I replied, smiling at him.

"Maybe even love me?"

"Love? This is only our second date, Cruise!" I couldn't believe my ears.

"Aha, so this *is* our second date! I knew it! You know what that means. What do you say? You ready for our third date? Life is short, you know."

"Is it?" I asked with a laugh and then paused to stare at him. "Once again you fail at asking me out."

"This again?" With a good-natured smile, he opened the top of my bottled Coke.

"Come by the house at seven and I'll give you my answer."

"Really?" he said with a bright smile, his playful dark eyes flashing with desire.

"Really. And for goodness' sake. Wear something nice."

The End

M. L. Bullock's Book List

If you think you've missed one of my books, here is a comprehensive list of everything.☺ All books are available on Amazon Kindle, and as paper books. Some are available as audiobooks.

SEVEN SISTERS

#1 Seven Sisters

#2 Moonlight Falls on Seven Sisters

#3 Shadows Stir at Seven Sisters

#4 The Stars That Fell

#5 The Stars We Walked Upon

#6 The Sun Rises Over Seven Sisters

#7 Beyond Seven Sisters

Bonus Christmas at Seven Sisters

Bonus The Ghost on the Swing

#8 Silent Night, Haunted Night

#9 Haunted Halls of Rosegate Manor

#10 Terror at Mossy Oak

#11 Dark Angel of Selma

The Ultimate Seven Sisters Collection

Seven Sisters Collection Vol. 1

Seven Sisters Collection Vol. 2

Seven Sisters Collection Vol. 3

IDLEWOOD

#1 The Ghosts of Idlewood

#2 Dreams of Idlewood

#3 The Whispering Saint
#4 The Haunted Child
The Hauntings of Idlewood
RETURN TO SEVEN SISTERS
#1 The Roses of Mobile
#2 All the Summer Roses
#3 Blooms Torn Asunder
#4 A Garden of Thorns
#5 Wreath of Roses
Return to Seven Sisters Collection
THE GRACEFIELD HAUNTINGS
#1 Haunted Gracefield
#2 The Three Graces
#3 Grace Before Dying
The Gracefield Hauntings Collection
MARIETTA
#1 The Bones of Marietta
#2 Footsteps of Angels
Marietta
THE BEAUMONT SAGA: A SEVEN SISTERS PREQUEL
#1 Olivia
#2 Louis
#3 Christine
The Beaumont Saga
DEVECHEAUX ANTIQUES AND HAUNTED THINGS
#1 A Cup of Shadows
#2 A Voice From Her Past
#3 A Watch of Weeping Angels
#4 The Ghost Mirror
#5 The Phantom Lamp
#6 The Darkening Door
#7 Kalliope's Dollhouse

#8 The Mourning Heart
Devecheaux Antiques and Haunted Things Trilogy Volume 1
Devecheaux Antiques and Haunted Things Trilogy Volume 2
SUGAR HILL
#1 Wife of the Left Hand
#2 Fire on the Ramparts
#3 Blood By Candlelight
#4 The Starlight Ball
#5 His Lovely Garden
The Sugar Hill Collection
THE GHOSTS OF SUMMERLEIGH
#1 The Belles of Desire, Mississippi
#2 The Ghost of Jeopardy Belle
#3 The Lady in White
#4 Loxley Belle
The Ghosts of Summerleigh
SOUTHERN GOTHIC SERIES
#1 Being With Beau
#2 Death's Last Darling
#3 Spook House
The Southern Gothic Collection
WELCOME TO DEAD HOUSE
#1 Never Dead
#2 Always Dead
#3 Dead at Midnight
Welcome to Dead House Series
HAUNTING PASSIONS
#1 For the Love of Shadows
#2 Her Haunted Heart
Haunting Passions
GULF COAST PARANORMAL Season One
#1 The Ghosts of Kali Oka Road

#6 The Spiritus Mirror
#7 The Captain of Water Street
#8 Return to the Leaf Academy
#9 The Rising of Lucy Vallow
Bonus Horror Ever After (A Gulf Coast Paranormal Extra)
GULF COAST PARANORMAL SEASON THREE
#1 Tower of Darkness
#2 Haunted Molly
#3 Dead Children's Playground
#4 The Malaga Demon
#5 A Hanging at Barton
#6 The Outlaw Screamer
TWELVE TO MIDNIGHT
#1 Mary Twelves
#2 Pieces of Twelves
BRYNN LEEDS HAUNTING
#1 We Walk in Darkness
MORGAN'S ROCK
#1 The Haunting of Joanna Storm
#2 The Hall of Shadows
#3 The Ghost of Joanna Storm
The Haunting at Morgan's Rock Trilogy
QUEEN MUMMY
#1 Queen Mummy
RIVER RUN
#1 River Run
#2 Blood Run
#3 Witch Child
River Run Collection
SOUTHLAND
#1 Southland
#2 Southland: Legacy

Southland: The Complete Collection
THE DESERT QUEEN
#1 The Tale of Nefret
#2 The Falcon Rises
#3 The Kingdom of Nefertiti
#4 The Song of the Bee Eater
The Desert Queen Collection
LOST CAMELOT
#1 Guinevere Forever
#2 Guinevere Unconquered
#3 The Undead Queen of Camelot
Lost Camelot Trilogy
SHABBY HEARTS (A Romantic Comedy Series)
#1 A Touch of Shabby
#2 Shabbier By the Minute
#3 Shabby By Night
#4 Shabby All the Way
#5 Star Spangled Shabby
#6 A Shabby Wedding
Shabby Hearts Collection
MISCELLANEOUS
Ghosts on a Plane
Dead Is the Loneliest Place to Be
After Ella
Ghosts of the Atlantis
BY MONICA BULLOCK
Delivered Me From Evil
ROSE FALLS
#1 Rose Falls
#2 Rose Shadows
#3 Rose Rising
Rose Falls Collection

THE NIKE CHRONICLES
Blue Water
Blue Wake
Blue Tide
The Nike Chronicles

Don't miss out!

Visit the website below and you can sign up to receive emails whenever M.L. Bullock publishes a new book. There's no charge and no obligation.

https://books2read.com/r/B-A-CXMC-WJPDF

BOOKS 2 READ

Connecting independent readers to independent writers.

Did you love *Blue Water*? Then you should read *A Touch Of Shabby*[1] by M.L. Bullock!

[2]

Arcadia Shabeaux can't believe her luck. Aunt Mavis hands her the keys to the family business, the Shabby Hearts Trailer Park and Campground, but there's a catch. It's only two weeks before tourist season begins and the place is in major disrepair.Lake Dennis isn't the hottest spot on the "Redneck Riviera," but Arcadia has plans to change all that. That is, if she can keep her dysfunctional family, a nosy Bigfoot and an overbearing television reporter in check.Add to the madness Arcadia's arrogant ex-boyfriend and an attractive newcomer who's caught her eye, and you've got a sure-fire recipe for disaster--and fun! When Pierre Ledbetter, the owner of the Happy Hooker Bait Shop, disappears, the residents of Shabby Hearts naturally blame it

---

1. https://books2read.com/u/3J606g

2. https://books2read.com/u/3J606g

on the legendary cryptid. Everyone except the sheriff, who believes a Shabeaux has to be responsible.The tension rises when a resident of the trailer park dies mysteriously and the Lake Dennis community erupts into chaos. Arcadia isn't sure how it will all play out, but she is determined to uncover the truth as quickly as possible. Immerse yourself in a humorous, small-town trailer park cozy mystery with a side order of the paranormal.

Read more at www.mlbullock.com.

About the Author

Author M.L. Bullock enjoys the laid-back atmosphere and the spooky vibe of the Gulf Coast, especially the region's historic districts and sites. When she isn't visiting her favorite haunts in New Orleans or Old Mobile, you can find her flipping through old photographs or newspaper clippings in search of new inspiration.

Read more at www.mlbullock.com.